D1167921

OUR LADY OF
ALL THE DISTANCES

OUR LADY OF
ALL THE DISTANCES

Elisabeth Harvor

HarperCollins*PublishersLtd*

Published by
HarperCollins Publishers Ltd
Suite 2900, Hazelton Lanes
55 Avenue Road
Toronto, Canada M5R 3L2

First Oberon Library edition
published May, 1991

Published by arrangement with Oberon Press

Canadian Cataloguing in Publication Data

Harvor, Elisabeth
   Our lady of all the distances

ISBN 0-00-617967-3

First Oberon Library edition
First published under title: Women & children.
I. Title. II. Title: Women & children.

PS8565.A6908 1991   C813'.54   C91-094240-4
PR9199.3.H3708 1991

91 92 93 94 95 96 OFF 10 9 8 7 6 5 4 3 2 1

OUR LADY OF
ALL THE DISTANCES

MONSTER BABY

"Babies are sometimes admitted," the lab technician told me, "with the diagnosis *failure to thrive*." She added that in the course of a day in the Hematology Department one encounters many strange diagnoses (only last week the staff had been perplexed by the diagnosis *hypomania*, a condition which, if the two sections of the word were literally translated, seemed merely to be the goal of the average man); such a non-thriving child, the lab technician said, was quickly visited by a phalanx of experts. Soon a corolla of concern would form around it: blood people, bone people, nutritionists, radiologists, psychiatrists, social workers, neurologists. She herself had sometimes felt a strong curiosity about their many reports, but had been reluctant to look at the charts for any reason that could not be justified on hematological grounds.

I asked her why.

She replied that she had always been led to believe that the charts belonged to the nurses. I told her that when I had been a nurse, a student nurse (before I had dropped out), I had always been led to believe that the charts belonged to the doctors. Together we marvelled at how easily we had been led to believe opposite things, and then we decided that the truth was the nurses were the guardians of the charts, but the doctors were the ones who owned them.

"Will you have another drink?" the lab technician asked me. "I'm going over to get myself one."

I handed her my glass. Then I watched her thread her way through the dancers, carrying the glasses, one in each hand, as if they were two tall black glass candles. Over at the table a thin pale man ladled out the punch for her. While he was doing this, I saw the lab technician glance over to where her husband was talking to a group of men. My eyes then searched out Karl. He was dancing with a plump woman with black hair and a black dress. The lab technician began to make her way back to where I was sitting. She was wearing a Chinese-style dress, a kind of heavy mauve silk dress that had what looked like sheaves of red wheat on it. Her straight blonde hair was pulled back in a bun, centre-parted, going black all along the centre line, like black grass that's been burned in the spring. She was very thin (this had puzzled me, for the thing we had discovered early in the evening was that we both suffered from a kind of metabolic disturbance that tends to make people fat; it's called hypoglycemia— it's the opposite of diabetes, it's also what generally precedes it; it has a whole repertoire of neurotic symptoms: migraine headaches, trembling, dizziness, depression; it was written up in the *Saturday Review* once, she told me, under the rather poignant title, *The Biochemistry of Anxiety*. Anxiety, in fact, is believed to be both cause and symptom—so much so that some doctors claim that the disease has been invented by the patients. These doctors have called hypoglycemia "the last refuge of the neurotic." But in answer to these doctors I've read scientists who've written about "ecological madness"—the environment backs up and causes diseases of metabolic imbalance. A kind of boomerang osmosis occurs: an unhealthy exchange between man and his world. The lab technician offered herself as a guinea-pig at the hospital where she works, but so far they've only asked her to take part in one

6

experiment, which turned out to be something of a disaster. It was an experiment to determine the effect of alcohol on people with low blood-sugar. They starved her for several hours, and when she arrived in the testing area the researchers, sounding like bar-girls, offered her a bewildering variety of drinks. She had just put in her order when it was discovered that the machine had broken down. She never did get her drink. Well, she's getting it now, I thought, watching her make her way over to me. She put a black glass in my hand and sat down beside me). It was somehow easy to imagine her in her working clothes, in a slightly soiled white lab coat, in sensible flat white shoes, her blood-sucker coiled in her pocket. It was a sleuth-like profession, I thought. It wasn't only in detective novels that blood was evidence. She told me about being on night duty. There were always three of them, usually girls—one from Hematology, one from Blood Bank, one from Biochemistry. Early in the evening they would check in with the hospital switchboard from the room in the psychiatric ward where they were allowed to spend the night. Then they would stretch out on the three beds, a kind of diagnostic blood trinity; the three graces, the three stooges, the three musketeers, the three bears. Between calls, they would sometimes sleep, dreaming strange dreams. During the day, the lab technician told me, the room was used as a recovery room for people coming out of electro-shock treatments. Perhaps that accounted for the strange dreams they had on night duty.

I smiled at her.

She smiled back at me, in a tentative way.

"I find it hard to imagine you as a nurse."

"Well, I was never a very good one. And I'm a painter now."

She wanted to know about my being a painter, what I painted, what it was like to paint. I tried to tell her, but all the time I was talking I was thinking about

7

being a student nurse, about the things that had happened. The two things that especially stood out in my mind seemed strangely connected: the birth of a baby that nobody wanted to live, and the death of a woman that nobody wanted to die. The monster baby was the child of the wife of one of the radiologists on staff. Rumours that the baby was a radiation mutation ran among the student nurses, but these rumours were quickly killed by the graduate nurses and doctors. Their denials implied that it was safer to believe in exceptions and bad luck than in cause and effect. As for the mother, she was never allowed to see the baby at all, it was considered so grotesque. She sat in her private room (blonde hair tied back with narrow brown velvet ribbon, baby roses nestling in ice chips), condemned to ignorance. Her baby's problem was not, like that of the lab technician's babies, a failure to thrive; its problem was a failure to die. It was transferred to the Contagious Diseases Annex, a lonely and isolated cinnamon-coloured building behind and below the main hospital. The main hospital was built on a rock—the Annex stood on the flat ground below it and had to be reached by a complex series of stairs and ramps on stilts. Doctors' orders said that the child was to receive no medication, no vitamins, no special care. The most rudimentary milk formula was prescribed. "We're only obeying orders," the student nurses said as they were preparing its rudimentary formula, and one of the supervisors had once remarked that "some kind soul should put arsenic in its milk." What the baby had instead was euthanasia in slow motion. And yet not euthanasia, since the quality of mercy had been drained from the act. The law (that life should not be interfered with) was grotesquely honoured—honoured to the point of perversion. It was difficult to feed the baby, I remember; its nose and mouth ran together, it had no brain. It had an elegant-sounding name—Penelope or Mariana or

8

Sophia. Its constitution was sadly, inappropriately sturdy: it took months to die.

Victoria Del Rio was in almost every way the baby's opposite: she was 47 years older than the baby and she was, besides, alert, dynamic and in proportion. She had thick hair, cut in a silver helmet, she wore peasant-style nightgowns of batiste with drawstrings at the neck and bordered with embroidered bunioned crosses made up of hundreds of little x's. She died, with neither panic nor fanfare, of cancer of the bladder. She died in great pain, as a matter of fact, but the doctor could only allow her to have morphine every four hours because of the narcotics laws. If she asked for injections oftener, and she sometimes did, she was to be given injections of sterile water (sterile placebos) for the doctor was prevented by law from turning her into a drug addict before she died. She hadn't been fooled by the injections of sterile water even though, in the syringe, they looked exactly like the injections of morphine. "I believe the doctor thinks I'm a hypochondriac," Victoria Del Rio once said to me. "It's not that," I said, in a moment of unprofessional candour, which was as good as admitting that the injections were half the time fake (and oh God, the relief to be able to admit it! Like performing last rites over the whole corpus of lies). "It's just that he has to obey the narcotics laws."

"Who was that you were talking to half the night?" Karl asked me as we were walking away from the party house. Inside the house people were still dancing. A garage light projected a cone of illuminated falling snow across the large rectangle of the window.
   "A lab technician from the Civic."
   "What were you talking about?"
   "Her work. My work."
   Her present. My past.

9

The wind made cold maps of pain on one side of my face, on the outside of one leg. We got into the car. I was remembering being on night duty in the Annex when It was there. When I fed It, It fitted into my arms like any other baby. It was a shock sometimes to have forgotten for a moment, and then to look down at It and see its perpetually swollen asymmetrical face. Nights were lonely in the Annex. There were usually only about ten patients there. They all remained separate from each other, the quarantine seemed to have extended even to the sound of their voices. In the evenings there were no visitors, no jokes, no calling back and forth. There were seldom even any flowers. It was a forgotten world. At midnight an orderly would appear with my dinner on a tray. He was a tired-looking man; it was said he had two jobs, he was a moonlighter, he worked daytimes in the Morgue. Sometimes, student nurses who had an hour off in the middle of the night would come down to see the monster baby. The students who were most interested were the ones from the Maternity Ward—the ones who knew its mother. Perhaps it was the sense of paradox that pulled them. Maybe they were wondering how a woman who looked like Miss Canada, Miss America, Miss World, Miss Universe (all the doctors' wives were like beauty queens; they had more flowers than the other patients, they were tanned even in winter, they had nightgowns that were so expensive they were purely white and simple—not shot through with eyelet, not frothed up with lace), maybe they were wondering how everyone's idea of an angel could give birth to a monster. I think I wondered it myself. I was too young and literal-minded to think in terms of allegory, but being a painter has sharpened my wits, has changed me. I can see the allegory now. I can see that any incident that has the right ingredients can represent the macrocosm. I can remember working in the Nursery. The Nursery, the Maternity Ward and the Case Room were the happy parts of the hospital. We used to sing when we worked in the Nursery, we used to sing at the tops of our lungs. "*There's a bright golden haze on the meadow*," we would shout, giving the babies their morning baths, creaming their newborn bodies with soap, spraying their newborn bodies with nozzles. And "*Ciao, Ciao, Bambino!*" we would cry fondly, fitting them fresh back into their drawer-like beds. The heavy soundproof doors that had been installed to deaden the squall of babies also deadened our daily celebration (through the songs of musical comedy) of life. Out on the ward things were pretty good too. Even the supervisor was happy. She made her rounds with her hands in the hip pockets of her uniform, she had freckles, she wore her cap shoved back on her head. And the mothers were happy. When we came around with the thermometers and wash-basins their pink-and-maroon plastic transistor radios were playing the highland reels of the breakfast shows. When we brought them their typical hospital breakfast (late) they didn't complain. Tea-pot stone cold. Steaming hot cream of wheat. A nicely warm and perfect egg. Two slices of cold dry toast. A tepid glass of grapefruit juice. They joked about their natural processes, they laughed at their nightgowns that were decorated like Rorschach blots with blood. They put on their chenille dressing gowns and went up to the Nursery window and asked to have their babies displayed. "He looks like a prize-fighter," they said, and "Oh look at that scowl, would you!" When their babies were brought in to them they said, "Hi, monster, how are things back at the ranch?" (Maybe they'd heard us singing after all, behind the Nursery doors, the songs from *Oklahoma*.)

One night when I was on my way to night duty in the Annex I walked through the Maternity Ward. I wanted to see Her, Its mother. She was just as pretty and wholesome as everyone had said she was. Perfect teeth. Eyes the right size. Hair from the shampoo ads. Nose from the ads for everything else. I still can't say whether I felt triumph or guilt or fear. I knew something that she didn't know, something that involved her. I had held the baby she had never seen, would never see; the baby that no-one could jokingly call "monster" because monster was what it was. I remember when the student nurses were first allowed out of the classroom and into the wards, I remember how we would smile when we would hear certain names called over the intercom, would smile when the magic name of "doctor" was paired with names like Fink, Hirt, Kronick, Rushforth and Crummey. But after a while it became apparent that there was no medieval morality play here: Dr. Kronick was not in chronic diseases, Dr. Rushforth, being a skin specialist, could hardly be expected to rush forth anywhere, Dr. Hirt was neither gentle nor brutal, Drs. Fink and Crummey were good doctors, nice guys. And in due time their names merged with names like McIntosh and O'Neill and Bannerman. So the morality play was elsewhere. Elusive. Everywhere. Out of reach. Earlier in the evening, when I was talking to the lab technician, I thought that what I was thinking about was very simple: lies versus truth. Simple. Victoria Del Rio and the monster baby's mother had both been protected from certain truths. The dignity of being allowed to come to terms with their situations had been denied them. But there was something else here. Something about interference. Some time earlier this evening I remember thinking in reference to the monster baby that the law (that life should not be interfered with) had been grotesquely honoured. But this was true only on the surface. Underneath the lack of interference there *was* interference. In the fabric of life there had been interference. In the mosaic of the blood something had been altered: the wrong chips were down. Maybe the baby was Miss World's baby or maybe it was even the baby of Miss Universe. It didn't know who it was. And neither did we. It didn't know it was a symbol. And neither did we. It didn't know how bad things could get. And neither did we. (After all, this was only in the fifties). For instance, it didn't know (and neither did we) that it had a good chance of appearing again in the thousands and hundreds of thousands; it didn't know (and neither did we) that it had a good chance of being born again.

PAIN WAS MY PORTION

They ate their picnics as they sat shored up against the graveyard wall—on the living side—with a view down into a far field where there were cows. Even from that distance they could see how the cows' fly-warding tails kept swinging with the languid regularity of bell-ropes, while much closer they could feel, warm and cracked at their backs, the sun-warmed cemetery wall.

Ralph's wife, Gladdie, always held her head high. It came, Ralph said, from an Edwardian childhood of too many blouses with high dog-collared collars, all in starched and unyielding cotton. Ralph had a theory about clothing styles changing the physiognomy of whole generations. "No receding chins in that era," he would say. And he liked to point out to Gladdie how her hair was always seeking its Edwardian beginnings—how no matter how tightly and classically she wound it up on top of her head in the mornings, it still, as the day wore on, worked itself out from its mooring of pins and became more Gibson Girlish. His own hair was in a silver brush-cut, his eyes were military-looking (they looked toughly into a secret distance), his clothes were in restrained colours, except for the one light touch of powder blue sneakers. In fact, most people hadn't even thought they were Americans when they had first come. Not by the way they dressed or talked. They weren't like the ones who came up with their loud plaids with voices to match.

The Fraziers, when they wore plaids, wore dark plaids that looked as if they had been steeped in pots of tea, and their specialty-shop sweaters looked as if they had been cut from hairy peat-bogs and had dull pewter buttons on them. And they were not wild pleasure-seekers either; they did research, their own project, supplying information from the gravestones of the Kingston cemetery to the Hampton Historical Society which, in an earlier summer, they had helped to found.

Their place of research was very windy and dry. The trees were too big. What had begun as shelter had ended as deprivation, and the graveyard lay like the environmental equivalent of a pale and over-protected child. It seemed as if the wind never stopped moving in the tops of the big trees—a wind that made the leaves fly-cast their spotted shadows across forgotten mounds and faded grass. But the Fraziers had been gradually changing all that. Even after heavy rains had pelted the graves with leaves ("like walking in wet cornflakes," Gladdie said), they were sometimes to be seen there, in milky plastic raincoats, gathering more evidence to help in the reconstruction of the history of the early community, kneeling to their researches like supplicants, tenderly feeling along the fronts of stones through crude pock-marks and embossed granite-coloured moss to find clues to names and dates. "A kind of braille in reverse," Gladdie called the incised letters. And on fine days they sometimes did charcoal rubbings. There was one verse that Gladdie particularly loved, one that she had made rubbings of for the kitchens of all her Boston friends:

PAIN WAS MY PORTION
PHYSIC WAS MY FOOD
CHRIST WAS MY PHYSICIAN
WHICH DID ME NO GOOD

They marvelled at the anger and the humour of it.

"Anger turned to humour," Ralph said, "by the alchemy of rhyme."

The early graves belonged mainly to United Empire Loyalist dead. That great exodus had long since reversed itself and gone back the way it came; now there was only the most irregular travel from south to north —made up of big loud prodigal sons who came to "Canader for the summah, Florider for the wintah," and who lived in places like Boston and Springfield in between; or there were the tourists who came up to the northeast coast of the continent for a quick change of country and a slightly cooler climate; or there were the draft dodgers and deserters whom the Fraziers didn't like to think about. They didn't approve of the war their government was fighting *either*, but they didn't think that dodging the draft should be necessary in a country that had universal suffrage. "*Universal suffrage?*" someone had cried, and when someone else had pointed out to them—and it was a Canadian who had pointed it out—that a boy could be shipped back home, neatly tucked in his coffin and wrapped in flags, long before he was ever old enough to vote, they had to agree; and when someone else, another Canadian (the Canadians were getting just as argumentative as the people back home) pointed out that the Loyalists had *also* been draft dodgers, the Fraziers had to agree again, but still *emotionally* they preferred those draft dodgers of the past, who had left their Georgian legacies along all the richest river valleys. A Canadian neighbour they had once been fond of made the mistake of saying that as a reason for not fighting in a war, the Fraziers preferred King to conscience. In self-defence the Fraziers decided that this man had become bitter and cynical. And so they continued annually to resolve their difficulties by trying to live, for the summer months of every year, not only in another country, but in another century of another country. Their summer house was an early Loyalist one, which they had got cheaply and restored expensively—though simply. Ralph would occasionally remark that it cost a lot to live such a simple life—as he scoured the countryside for early maple and butternut cabinets to use as fronts for electric dishwashers and hi-fi equipment. In fact, the twentieth century ran through the house in hidden veins of pipes and wires, not talked about, but *there*, like a crude word for a functional thing. On the surface though, everything was "period." They had found a Boston store that carried black and brown gingham wallpapers and fabrics of early prints. They had found early glass for the windows and early brick for the stairs, so that even if they suffered from astigmatism as they looked out at the brilliant mornings, even if they felt as if the stairs would crumble beneath them as they ran down into the brilliant mornings, they could still assure themselves that the reproduction they lived in was a faithful one.

Marian was their only child and had been born late in their marriage. She was a sad-necked girl with long, weakly gold hair and poor eyesight. Gladdie didn't like glasses (she was a tyrant for the natural) and she would frequently lift the glasses from the face of her pale helpless-eyed Botticelli daughter and advise her to go to her room and practice her eye exercises. When the eye exercises didn't seem to make an improvement, she thought of various compromises—having the glasses attached to black velvet reins, or to a chain of braided human hair so that they could hang down on the front of the bosom ("*What bosom?*" Marian had asked) and be swung up to the eyes in times of emergency. Marian, who still had a small guilty residue of respect for the opinion of her peers, carried the glasses in the pocket of her jeans. Gladdie didn't care about Marian's peers. Or their opinions. The ones in Boston were too fast; the ones in Hampton were too dull. In fact, what connection these empty-eyed teenagers had with their salty keen-eyed grandparents, Gladdie simply could not see. In two generations—and in some cases, one—all the naturalness had been drained from these people; she could not imagine any robust haystack sex preceding the large annual yield of illegitimate babies; instead, she thought of the girls lying obedient and dull as cows in the backs of cars, their white thighs flopped open, their eyes looking up at nothing, even at the height of the act, chewing gum. Chewing cuds! (When Ralph listened to Gladdie lamenting the passing of robust haystack sex, he kept his mouth shut. A gentleman never tells, he thought, giving that old saw a new, piquant and strangely opposite meaning, for only he was in the unfortunate position of knowing that Gladdie's sexuality was locked back in the eighteenth century— like her taste.) And the clothes they wore! Gladdie went on. She had seen them at the Saturday night dance wearing rhinestone imitations of the Queen of England's necklaces (and the Queen of England's taste was certainly nothing to stand up and cheer about) and dresses made from maroon taffeta with a large grain in it like plywood. Their teeth had potato-eyes in them from what she imagined to be a constant diet of root beer and lime rickey—that is, the ones who *had* their teeth, for it was their collective ambition (and probably, Gladdie thought, the only ambition they had ever had) to have all their teeth pulled out by the time they were twenty. She averted her eyes from them in embarrassment and pain—she loved "character" and "naturalness," and she tried to make Marian see how wrong they would be as friends. "But what about the kids in Boston?" Marian had asked. "*They're* natural." And she thought of the kids of Boston, the girls without make-up and wearing long hair and faded pants. Or else they wore short calico dresses, demure, high-necked, smocked. Gladdie saw red when she thought of those cocoa, blue and slate-coloured dresses that were made of calico patterns appropriated from the eighteenth and nineteenth centuries and cut off at thigh length. They reminded her, she said, of Georgian houses cut down into ranch style. And this was how she won all the arguments. With her perfect taste and her feeling for the authentic. "And the kids in Boston have no *character*," Gladdie told Marian. "They have poor posture and no ambition." And so Marian, who also had poor posture and no ambition, went everywhere with her parents: to timeless afternoon teas with two old sisters in their high old house at the helm of a large loose garden, to the sour parlours of people too proud to go to nursing homes, to endless mornings on the sunken verandahs of the town characters, for long country drives hunting down Canadiana, on picnics, and to the graveyard near Kingston.

Marian's memories of the graveyard were both peaceful and bizarre. Most of her childhood seemed to have been spent there among its moss-mottled stones and she could remember strange (strange because so casual) meals eaten at a large family gravestone made in the shape of a table, accommodating at least six people above ground and what appeared to be a whole dynasty below. She seemed to remember ham sandwiches being carefully divided out over IN LOVING MEMORY OF, and milk spilled on dark eroded stone, and the careful recording of how long the people had lived, how long outwitted a cruel fate, not just the pathetically meagre years only, but often the more generous months and days as well. But then with Marian memory often lacked the quality of an accurate recording of events, and seemed sometimes to be imagination in retrospect.

But as the years passed by, the Fraziers spent less time in the Kingston graveyard. Their passion for Loyalist statistics gradually became sated, they became preoccupied with the restoration of their house, and they often had long visits from American friends.

The summer Marian was fourteen, Esther Abrams

came to visit. None of the Fraziers had ever met her before she came, but they felt as if they had known her for years for she was the sister of one of their oldest friends, Helen Helpmann. They had got a letter from Helen early in July asking if it would be all right if she and Esther arrived the following week. Esther was sick, Helen wrote, so they were taking the plane rather than the train for reasons of comfort. Also to save time: for Helen also wrote that the doctor had given Esther four—at the most, five—more months to live. The Fraziers rose to the challenge of this disheartening news, terribly aware of its irony. They had wanted for years to meet Esther, and now at last their wish was going to be granted, and they would all meet, only to know that they would never meet again. It had the boomerang quality, the malevolent charity with which wishes are granted in fairytales, and Gladdie lamented for Esther, for Esther's husband, for Helen, for themselves, as she cheered up the room at the top of the stairs. She rounded up the brightest-coloured cushions from the other bedrooms and unpacked the red and white quilt made by the Ladies' Aid. She took down "Pain was My Portion." She took down a Currier & Ives engraving called "The Farewell" and put a Dufy poster in its place. She imagined the kinds of flowers she would pick, not the heavy-scented creamy ones like peonies and roses, but molecular peppery ones—Queen Anne's Lace, caraway, lupins—and vigorous ones—tiger lilies, Devil's Paintbrushes—all gathered into gay improbable bouquets. She took Marian aside and explained about the cancer, that it was incurable, that Esther Abrams herself knew she was going to die.

"We'll try to make it a very happy visit, dear, and I want you to know the facts about it so you don't start talking about cancer or dying or anything like that."

And then, propelled by her own kind of tense

bustle, she was off to the clothesline with a pan of washing. Marian came down the steps after her, and stood watching.

"Where is it, Mother?"

"Where's what?"

"The cancer."

Gladdie pegged the last sheet to the line, then rolled the pulley out. It was one of her limitations that she frequently found the truth to be in bad taste. "There is nothing they can do," she said, hoping *that* would do.

"But *where* is it?"

"Last year she had a breast removed," Gladdie said in a far-off voice; "they thought they'd got it all out, but they hadn't."

Marian continued to stand there, waiting.

The sheets, filled with wind, moved in solemn columns.

"There's nothing more to *tell*," Gladdie said sharply; "go to your room now, and tidy it up."

Much as they may have felt prepared for Esther, the Fraziers were all surprised by her. She seemed so incredibly alive, and for a woman who had only four months to live, she seemed very sure of herself. And she had big breasts. Marian was cross with herself when she realized how much this surprised her. Surely she hadn't expected her to come with one half of her bosom limp and flat like a war-amputee with his empty flat sleeve tucked into his pocket. How stupid can you be! she thought sternly to herself. Still, she found herself keeping her eyes carefully averted from Esther Abrams' breasts, and even from her face.

"Dear, *try* to be a little more *natural*," her mother said to her one afternoon, giving her a fiercely reassuring smile.

"Yes, Mother," Marian said, sighing heavily, walking up the stairs—Yes mother, yesmother, yesmother, yesmother.

She did soon become more relaxed, though. It was Esther who did it. She put them all at their ease, all of them, even Marian. "She's remarkable!" Gladdie and Helen were constantly reminding each other, in their new, low, charged voices, even when they could see Esther through the kitchen window far off in the field picking wild flowers, even when they knew she was far away at the beach, they spoke in their new low voices. They would do anything not to be her, anything. Bestow any praise, renounce any pleasure. They spent their days conspiring diversions: trips, picnics, bonfires, charades. And Esther tried not to be one of those tiresome invalids who never needs anything done for her. She allowed herself to need almost everything, the hot toddies at night, the warm pine baths in the later afternoon, the wild batik of Gladdie's made up into an amusing dressing-gown, the impulsive flights into town to see the grade-B movies that they snorted over like demented teenagers, the back-rubs, the rests after lunch. And Gladdie put a great deal of love and care into the meals. Breakfast was made to be Edwardian-ample with omelets and bread dipped into eggnog and fried, with Scottish marmalades, English jams, Oriental and South American teas. Sometimes they let breakfast go on for hours. They told a lot of stories and laughed a lot and were afraid of silences. Every breakfast was distinguished by the desperate gaiety of the Titanic going down. It was as if they were trying to pretend they could control time, but in the end, thought Marian, anxious to go swimming, they only wasted it.

Marian came to idolize Esther. "Esther down yet?" was the first thing she would say when she came down to breakfast in the mornings, and "Where's Esther?" when she came in from swimming in the afternoon— "Esther in?" Gladdie and Helen both noticed how Marian adored Esther. And one day when Gladdie was puttering in her room, Marian came by. She was on her way to the neighbours' to get some eggs. She needed money from her mother, got it, then hesitated a moment. Gladdie was wearing a sensible black bathing suit, but she was one of those fortunate people on whom the sensible looks classic.

"What is it?" she asked her daughter. Marian had been looking pale lately, she thought.

"I was wondering."

"What is it? What were you wondering?"

"Something about Esther."

Gladdie listened for a moment, in the direction of downstairs, with her eyes.

"Are they all out?"

Marian nodded.

"Well?"

"I was wondering what kind of padding she puts in it—I mean in the other half of her brassiere."

Gladdie looked shocked. Looking shocked was a ploy she had occasionally used with children. All parents do, she imagined. Nice people don't ask such things, her look said.

"Oh well," said Marian, defeated, "I just wondered . . . ," and she went down the hall and slowly descended the stairs in a series of sad little hops.

"Marian." Her mother's voice, behind and above her. Her mother was standing on the landing. Her high blades of cheekbones looked polished—she must have been creaming her face. She towered there at the stair top, an icon in a channel swimmer's bathing-suit. And, "She has a kind of foam-rubber pad built into her brassiere," she said, quickly, like a child saying something she's been dared to. And at that moment the broad handsome planes of her face fragmented, buckled up, became a terrible terrain of fear, of terror. She jerked her face away from Marian so that her own daughter would not see the shame of her fear, and went quickly down the hallway to her room.

Marian fitted the money into her pocket and just

23

before she stepped out into the sun, she cupped her hands under her own small breasts. Then she deftly darted her blouse into her shorts and started off for the next farm. Lately she had begun to wake up at night, needing to use the toilet. She didn't try to discover why (too much cocoa? too few blankets?) and so prevent its recurrence; she only stumbled, bewildered but dutiful, downstairs to the bathroom, then upstairs again and at once back to sleep. One night though, she made the mistake of trying to orient the sky to the night (is it near morning? she wondered) and she made her way through wicker mounds to one of the sunporch windows. It had turned cold for summer and although the hills around the house were dark, the sky was not very dark, it was medium blue. But cold. And speckled with stars. Everyone's asleep, she thought, the living and the dying. Those words "the living and the dying" came to her without warning and they filled her with such immediate and spontaneous terror that her only thought then was to get upstairs as fast as she could, and she fled to the stairway. And all the way up it was as if a powerful hand was clutching for her ankle, filling her legs with tremors so that thrills of terror ran down them, so that they seemed to have the consistency of running water, like legs in dreams. At last she got to her room, got the door closed tight behind her, stood leaning hard against it, everything roaring and pounding inside her. "Ideas rose up in crowds," she thought, remembering a line from a book in her father's study. And that quickly turned into "ideas rose up in shrouds." She had always been able to terrorize herself by rhyme. And she had kept the light on till morning that night; it wasn't till the sun rose and began to fill her room with pallid early life that she had finally fallen asleep.

A few days before Esther and Helen were due to leave, Gladdie got saddled with some kind of committee meeting at her house, and she suggested that the two of them go off for a drive and take Marian along as their guide. "Esther looks tired," Gladdie said in a low voice to Helen. Esther, coming down the stairs in a dark wool skirt and a blue sweater, did not look especially tired, but there was, among the others, almost a ritual of anticipating exhaustion on her behalf. Marian ran up to her room for her cardigan, and when she came down again the three of them set off on the north-bound road out of Hampton. Sussex, "the dairy-centre of the Maritimes" according to the map, did not particularly entice them, and soon after they left Hampton they turned left and took the road down the Kingston Peninsula. Marian suggested they visit the old Merritt-Wetmore house, now restored, and once the home of one of the first Loyalist families in the district. Tea was served there too, Marian said. It had started to rain. They decided to go to the Merritt-Wetmore house. The black car moved under a roof of dripping leaves and came, beaded with black rain, out into the open near Kingston.

They found the house and looked around and had their tea. When they came back to the car, there was a long glaring underbelly to the navy sky—did it mean more rain or did it mean clearing? It had turned cold, it seemed like a day in October. They got into the car and started out toward Hampton.

"What church is that?"

"The Kingston Anglican church. We can turn left here, if you'd like to see it."

Helen turned left and they soon swung in beside it. Their thighs felt stuck together, their legs stiff. They got out. It was curious, Marian thought, she had not been down here since last year, and now the church looked dilapidated, blotched with rain. The paint had mostly worn off, what was left was flaky silver, and the stained-glass windows, so gaudy from the inside, only looked black from the outside, and a little rough, like black water the wind had lightly blown over.

They went inside. In there it smelled of the sweet damp of an old and closed building. It had some hideous bits all right (the Victorian windows donated in advance by wealthy parishioners in memory of themselves, for instance), but on the whole it was a beautiful building. "Preserved in a state of original sin through lack of funds for modernization," was what Ralph always said about it, adding that he would contribute only to its upkeep, but never to its renovation. He had even composed a small prayer that contained the words, "Preserve us, O Lord, from marbled arborite and chrome." Marian quoted this, and the two women smiled. They came outside, blinking in the strange after-rain light.

Marian led them into the churchyard and showed them the tombstone with the angel smoking a pipe, and the lovely sentimental ones with weeping willows, and the ones with shapely limp hands laid over roses. Then there were the six little Elizabeths all in a row, all daughters of one of the early ministers of the church. It was a rather terrifying case of stubborn optimism, Marian explained. He had named his first daughter Elizabeth and when she had died as an infant, the second-born child had been named after her, and so on right through the sixth birth and death. A man who had refused to be intimidated by omens, and who had lost. That was how Ralph had put it, anyway. And at the end of the row was the father's own grave and the grave of his wife who, after such an orgy of tragedy, had also died young. Marian took them to the knoll where the tombstone in the shape of a table was, and she pointed out to them the four table legs made in the shape of burial urns, then she led them down into the lower reaches where she found and read aloud the inscription beginning "Pain was my portion." After a little searching she was also able to locate the grave of the Wetmore who had built the house they had visited earlier in the afternoon.

"Well! And where all did you go?" Ralph asked as they sat down to supper that night. Helen said that they had gone down the peninsula and had visited the Merritt-Wetmore house. And she immediately launched into a discussion of the house and its chairs: Hitchcock, thumb-back, Acadian. Marian was waiting for a chance to add that they had also visited the Kingston church, and was just on the point of saying so when it suddenly struck her: she shouldn't have taken Esther there! Oh God, don't let Helen tell Mother, was all Marian could think, all through the meal, please God, please God, please.

And that night she watched them, kneeling to her low bedroom window. She was wearing one of her mother's long satin nightgowns—this one had insets of beige lace and a beige lace butterfly appliquéd on it close to the ankle. Not for her the baby-doll pyjamas of her peers. And down below her, down in the garden, down by the pond where the singing of the frogs was like beeps from outer space, the two women, Gladdie and Helen, walked, their arms linked, murmuring like doves in their houndstooth checked slacks. She wondered what they were saying, but all the same she was grateful that she didn't have to know.

The day that Esther and Helen left was one of tense ebullience. Ralph and Gladdie had anticipated, they felt, all the emotional snags, and with a loving cunning circumvented them all. They had got presents for both but the presents had been hidden in the car to be saved for the airport—for the last ten minutes before take-off. They presented Helen with hers first: a buxom velvet box. "Oh you shouldn't have—" she had already started to say, before opening it, and when she did undo the clasp, expecting as she said later, "a diamond necklace at the very least," a jack-in-the-box green monster leaped out, causing all the grown-ups to shriek and roar till tears streamed down their faces. It was Esther who in the end got the necklace—

27

a nice silver one, simple and tasteful (but that's what people say about gravestones, Gladdie thought, struck with horror)—for they had decided against liquor or perfume since both so obviously lacked permanence, and the necklace was given to Esther in an immense cardboard carton. She had to go through what appeared to be a year's supply of newspapers to reach it at the bottom and this caused more hilarity, and a general need for drinks. "Thy word is a lamp unto my feet," Ralph said ringingly, when his wife, according to plan, expressed a desire for drink, and he pulled a thermos up from the picnic basket, and some paper cups. "The man who thinks of everything," he said, handing the cups around. He even gave one to Marian. "Learn now, pay later," he said, although "Fly now, die later," was the horrible counter-slogan that hovered immediately unbidden in his mind. The drink was quite weak, concocted to get them over the worst, but not of a strength to start crying-jags.

Esther did not die in four months after all, or in five. After she had got back to Seattle she was put on a new drug which for a while seemed to hold her disease stable—for a while she even seemed to improve, but toward the end of winter whatever hold the new drug had had weakened, and she was put into hospital. Her husband and Helen and Helen's husband spent many hours of every day there with her, for her condition was now so serious that there were no visitors' restrictions. The room seemed to Helen like a starched white apron seen through a thick lens; white light hitting so much white linen and bouncing off and welling round so many glass and chromium fittings. The only human thing about it was the smell of dying, not quite hidden under the stepped-up smell of ointment and flowers. And Esther was like a child in her johnny-shirt—sickness and institutions had brought out the waif in her—and yet not like a child at all, but like a figurehead, a woman at the prow of her pain. It was only in the movement of the legs that the pain showed, her legs were restless in the bed, bending and straightening and bending again, forever moving in the small sea of her bed, as if through the agency of her legs she was trying to dissipate her pain. And so up there, in the top of the hospital, in Esther's glass and chromium shrine, the level in the intravenous bottle kept dropping like the level of sand in an hourglass—even that, even the intravenous that was supposed to prolong her life, reminding them, with every drop, how her life was running out.

That summer the Fraziers went to Hampton as usual. While they were there, early in July, a letter came from Seattle. Gladdie opened it, then went immediately into the back garden to find Ralph.

"Ralph!" she called in an urgent disintegrating voice, "Ralph!" He turned and saw her face, her eyes like flags of pain. "Esther?" She nodded and he came to her and took her in his arms. After a little while they went in to make themselves tea, then carried the lukewarm cups, shaking in their saucers, out to the garden. They cried as they drank. Even when you expected it, it was still terrible.

"Poor Marian, I hope she doesn't take it too hard."

"Where is she?"

"Gone into town. To the store."

"Well maybe you'd better go to meet her; that way she'll know something's up."

But Marian, turning into the long laneway from the main road saw only that her mother was coming to meet her. She didn't know that something was up. She waved to Gladdie. Gladdie raised her arm in a stiff salute, then let if fall abruptly to her side.

"I think I remembered everything!" Marian called.

Gladdie came up to Marian and took her free arm and without saying anything began to walk with her.

"Something's wrong," Marian said, after a few minutes.

"We got a letter from Helen. Esther's . . . gone."

Marian didn't cry after all. All afternoon her parents kept plying themselves with tea, kept reaching over and clasping hands, kept looking, Marian thought, like thunderstruck spaniels. Finally she took a walk to the field and took a book with her. And for a long time she sat up on the field hill, stubble piercing her bum, trying to remember what Esther looked like. But she could call forth no clear image of Esther. The shock of a sudden visual image hadn't jelled; maybe she'd looked at Esther too steadily instead of being surprised into remembering her. There were so many other things she *could* remember. She could remember the first day Esther had come and how they were showing her her room, she could remember how off and on all that afternoon wide bands of dark had been moving down across the hills whenever clouds crossed the sun. And while they'd been showing it to her, Esther's room was suddenly steeped in dark. Then everyone had started to talk at once, a bad sign, always, and then, after what had seemed forever—ten seconds? fifteen?—the sun had come out again, and the lace-like flowers seemed made of sun and fire, and the red and white quilt from the Ladies' Aid shone out with its ritual backwoods geometry. "What a marvellous room," Esther had said, taking it all in. And then Marian remembered how sometimes when she had been younger and they had been doing research at the Kingston graveyard (her father, her mother, herself) how sometimes there would have been a new death, a fresh grave, and they would never work near it, wanting to keep their distance from it, with its harsh green raffia square of fake grass on it, not colour-co-ordinated to the real grass but looking like a scatter-rug on the great tawny dried-up floor of the cemetery.

Supper that night was late. It was a convalescents' supper—more tea of course, and cold leftovers from the fridge. Every man for himself. Gladdie was feeling very upset about Marian's lack of sorrow. She remembered what Helen had told her about Marian taking her and Esther to the Kingston cemetery and dragging them over every inch of consecrated ground. An exhaustive guided tour of the dead. And a strange business too. The phrase "psychiatric help" had been mentioned between them, rather tentatively at the time. Now Gladdie looked at her daughter with shrewd anxiety.

Marian helped with the supper dishes, then said she was going upstairs to bed. It was late to be finishing dishes, after ten. "I seem to have lost all sense of time," Gladdie said, leaning into her husband's embrace. He kept patting her on the back. As if losing all sense of time was some sort of achievement. Marian, making no comment, and no comment was disapproval enough, climbed the stairs. Through the open window she could hear how the eleven-and twelve-year-olds were singing down on the beach. They were singing "Red Sails in the Sunset," dragging the words so slowly over the melody that the melody was lost almost entirely. In another year or two they would be able to go to the Saturday-night dances and dance to it. "Red Sails in the Sunset" was what was always played for the final dance of the night. "A dirge in three-quarter time," was what Ralph usually called it, trying to make Marian feel better about not being one of the crowd. Walking along the upstairs hall, Marian could hear the singing quite clearly, all the way up from the beach.

Gladdie soon detached herself from Ralph and went up the stairs. "Marian?" she said, outside her door. "Okay if I come in for a minute?" Oh it was hard, raising daughters. Hard.

"Sure."

Marian was sitting on her bed, unbuttoning her blouse. What a closed expression her face has! Gladdie thought, alarmed.

"Marian."

"Yes, Mother?"

"Esther was very fond of you."

Like a vulture for grief, her mother seemed to her now, with her bright prominent eyes fixed on her in a hard assessing way.

"Yes, I know."

But Marian couldn't cry. Gladdie stood in the doorway a little longer, then it became awkward, her being there, and neither of them saying anything. "Good-night, then." But I am disappointed in you, her eyes said.

"Good-night, Mum."

After Gladdie had left, Marian folded her blouse and shorts and put them on a chair. Then she leaned over and unhooked her brassiere, a precious extra thing to put on and take off (since last month). As its straps slid down her arms, she suddenly felt the most intense burning pain in her throat. She lay down, pulled the sheet up to her armpits, then lay still as a statue on the catafalque of her bed. The moonlight drained her arms of tan. And her long burning painful column of neck kept separating her stony head from her anguished heart.

LIES IN SEARCH
OF THE TRUTH

I'm a poor driver and have picked a perfect night to prove it. It's raining very hard and it's also cold so that the streets are like black grease. It must have started while we were in the clinical limbo of Supermart Haven picking up our weekly supplies, must have come in over the dark city in a great invasion of dancing bouncing needles while we, all unaware, were hesitating over our choice of out-of-season fruit displayed in the square nests of green raffia, or while the children were fighting over what brand of breakfast cereal to buy. They choose them on the basis of the "free gifts." BOYS AND GIRLS! the packages cunningly exhorted my children from their upper left-hand corners, BUILD YOUR VERY OWN SUPERSONIC TRANSPORT! And from their lower right-hand corners they cried: GARÇONS ET FILLETES! CONSTRUISEZ VOTRE AVION DE TRANSPORT SUPERSONIQUE! Then we came out into this movie-style downpour—tropical in intensity but cold in temperature. After all, it is November, and Canada is not a hot country even at the best of times.

Lower down, the streets have been turned into instant black rivers and my eyes are aching as the windshield wipers make and remake their insistent perfect fans on the beaded glass. I can remember reading a review of a book by Françoise Sagan. As proof that Miss Sagan could still write, the reviewer lifted a little scene from the book telling of a woman who is driving away in her car after leaving her lover. It's not raining but the woman has turned the windshield wipers on. In a moment though, she realizes her mistake, realizes that it's she who is crying, not the sky, and she turns the windshield wipers off. She could cry and thought it rained. I know it rains but cannot cry. Although I can feel uncried tears like burning upward arrows in my throat. Pointing the way to my eyes, their exit. But there is no exit. A whole chin-up, socks-up past has built detours so involuted that the eyes are never reached. The eyes as an exit are out of bounds. On the day it happened I cried though, I'll say that for myself. And although I will continue to wish forever that we had cried together, rubbing our wet blind faces against each other like two gentle star-crossed animals, bone against bone, eye against crying eye, long hair combed by seeking unshaven jaw, in fact I did not cry until the end of that sucked-out moment after he had gone. But that was two weeks ago. I haven't cried since.

In the back seat the children have already started to fight over the free gifts. Family fights have erupted over these worthless plastic tokens, in our house and probably in countless other houses across this and other nations. And car accidents have no doubt also been caused. Maybe even deaths have occurred. Those cereal manufacturers have a lot to answer for. And fights or no fights, rain or no rain, night driving is difficult for me. I cannot easily find the traffic lights among all the commercial on-again-off-again ones, my eyes are too easily lured by the lights running like something crazed around the movie-house marquees, by the frenzied mysterious assessments in the tall thin sticks that quickly fill and refill with red and silver bands of neon (barometers, thermometers), by the way all the trundled lights combine to flee along the dark night bodies of the cars.

But now the fighting seems to be over, and ten

years of motherhood have taught me that there can only be a sinister reason for this. At the first traffic light I strain to listen, and hear a sound born to chill a mother's heart. It sounds like cornflakes leaking in a bountiful stream from a torn cereal box. And it sounds as if it will go on forever. Images of wood shavings being shot down the chutes of sawmills come to mind. But now it *has* stopped. A hand must have been clapped over the offending hole. There is absolute silence back there. Maybe guilt will unite the warriors. Maybe guilt will keep them quiet till we all get home.

In the morning I should vacuum the car. Should but probably won't. I'd like to take to heart Flaubert's advice: "Be regular and ordinary in your life, like a bourgeois, so that you can be violent and original in your works." Perhaps I flatter myself that it's only the first part of these instructions I would have trouble with. In any case Flaubert's advice will console me as I compile the weekend stew and make the beds (moving down in the hierarchy from king-size to camp cot), but it won't help me much as I find myself pushed toward the end of the day without having had a chance to paint. But weekends, so beloved of the children, must be accepted philosophically. After all, the whole week while they're at school, I have my secret life: I can paint as much as I like.

For my work I wear a pair of Lewis' old gold corduroy pants tied around the waist with a piece of gold curtain cord that ends in tassels, an old patterned shirt from which the brown and purple strength has been sapped by washings and sunnings, my black hair knotted back in a black chiffon scarf. Painters' clothes. Flaubert would not approve. I don't think he would approve of the clothes I wear at other times either. But if Flaubert were alive today, he probably wouldn't have any choice. It has become bourgeois to be bizarre. One has only to go into Supermart Haven on a crowded Friday night in midsummer to see that violence and originality have been appropriated by the textile designers. Violence anyway. I don't suppose that originality, by its very nature, can be appropriated by anyone. As for me, I have discovered if I wear skirts and sweaters, I am simply a haggard woman, but if I put on a batik shift, say, or if, for a party, a black blouse with an evening skirt made out of Balinese fabric, presto! my bones acquire planes and shadows. I also keep a drawer filled with earrings made of dismantled chandeliers, Cleopatra necklaces made of rosary beads and other crowd-pleasers, and if some women are able to say of their clothes, "I made it myself," I am able to say the same thing of my jewelry. There is one African print dress that I especially like, it is mostly browns and blacks and blues, it is really quite horrible if you look at it closely, it has what look like little shrines or torches in white on black with flaming red haloes around them, and what look like little drops of blood falling through the black and brown cross-hatching, and it has gone funny a few places from the wash and has turned here and there a cloudy dark blue, but the whole effect is very splendid. Although Johnnie told me once that all the African textiles are made in England—in Manchester or Birmingham or someplace like that, but I think he told me that when I was wearing the African print dress and he wanted me to take it off and go to bed with him. Driving in the car makes me want him more than ever. I want to open to him all ways, all over. And now that he's gone it seems there's no word to cover the feeling of loss. As if I were the only person to feel the limitations of the language! The limitations of the language must be felt in *all* the languages. And yet it was a mutual loss and one we decided on together. For over a year we had an easy arrangement. I wasn't possessive or demanding. Not on the surface anyway. Whenever he arrived on the scene I was grateful, and the times he couldn't come I had the paintings to work on, or the children to run with in the battered wilds of our local park. In these park-memories it seems the children and I (was it their bubbling laughter that made it seem this way?) were being funnelled down the steep slope like the Assyrian hordes —or was it the Abyssinian hordes—anyway, like the hordes, and my memory of it is that we were running down through the narrowing gap between the trees, bright tumbling sweaters doused by the sudden shadow of the funnel-stem part of the path. In those days it seemed that what was going on between Johnnie and me might go one forever. He was more interested in my work than any husband would ever be. But I don't know how it was with his own wife. He showed me a photograph of his house and his wife once. The house was an old Victorian brick one, and his wife was looking out of one of the windows—like a port-hole it was, this window—a Victorian oval port-hole. And somehow the shape of this window dates her, puts her back in the past where I want her, so that in some gallery of my mind she hangs forever immobile, stuck in a golden oval frame. And held in that imagined rim she is in the mud, flesh, black and dusty-theatre-curtain colours of Modigliani, and she has sagging oval eyes. Looking into those dark remembered ovals, I cannot believe what all the "other woman" women before me have been unable to believe—that the wife deserves or understands the husband.

I remember clearly the day that signalled the end for Johnnie and me, although neither of us seemed to know it at the time. *In fact, at the time* ("in fact, at the time," being the great and bewildered clarion call of hindsight), it seemed that that particular day signalled the beginning of a very deep level of connection between us. I had been painting and Johnnie had come by, and I had made him some tea, and we had sat drinking it close beside each other, and as I walked across the room to the sink I was aware of Johnnie's eyes holding on like strong hands to my hips, then I was standing at the work-sink rinsing out the brushes, shaking the warm drops in strong unison from both tea cups and brushes, when suddenly I said something, said a phrase which had formed itself a thousand times in my mind, but which I had planned, had vowed, never to say. I said, "I want to be your wife." I surprised even myself, saying anything about wanting to be his wife. I had always thought it was allowable to think but not to say. So possessive. Not smart. Johnnie's face is reprinted permanently in some kind of recollecting eye-bank in the back of my mind. Anytime I want I can summon up his face as it looked then, at that moment. His face was shocked, but not with anger or disgust. All those film sequences that show close-ups of lovers' faces moving toward each other—the faces move as if the bodies are swimming—there is a kind of accuracy about them . . . time and distance definitely get shaken up. Then the ego boundaries are broken in a cinematic dissolve. And there's something to be said for the authenticity of the following blackout too. I always used to think it was for the censors, but now I know a blackout represents part of what's really happening. Unless of course it's for the censor who resides within. My children came home, into all of this, we heard their troop-like feet on the outside stairs, and we stood up, hiding our hands in our pockets, waiting for the once-over. But the children came in with their desperate need to eat and pee, they hardly noticed us at all. Their preoccupation with intake and output condemned us to a surprised, uneasy safety.

But about that other, oh sweet God, I can still see Johnnie's face, anytime I want I can run that reel over. From the blackout there are still images I am recovering though (do I recover them or do I invent them?), there are still days when I want to sit and nurse my memories and not work or anything. Days when I want to sit and fish, a look here, a word there, the memory of the slow hand of love (his, mine, what does it matter?) moving from the gentle crater of the eye down to the centre of the world. And there are other days when I work like a madman, when even the time it takes to make myself a tunafish sandwich seems like the most monstrous outside interference. Days when hot golden broth with islands of fat-skin floating in it stands peaceful, untouched, on the stove. When I got married I thought I knew everything. I thought I knew what it was to be vulnerable, for instance, for I had been lonely and had needed to use the toilet in all the major cities of Europe. I had worked as a typist in London, as a waitress in France, and had nearly starved on the Costa Brava. I could speak two languages and could sing love songs in a third. But before I knew Johnnie did I know anything about laying myself on the line? On the bed, yes. On the line, no. But after that afternoon my feelings for him got very intense. We tried to see each other very often. Or that was the illusion. Maybe I wanted to see him often and he was really beginning to back away from me and tried to see me often in order to cover up. In any case, our work suffered. Johnnie was working on a film about emotionally disturbed children and he was not giving it the time it needed. The figures in my paintings waited for me to change or finish them. And our relationship also waited. Waited for us to change or finish it. So suppose we got married, we reasoned, it might cure the intensity of our feeling for each other (there was a statistically whopping chance of that) but did we want to be cured? And what about the children? we asked each other. And what about my husband Lewis? His wife Solange? Old-fashioned questions, all of them, when all around us families were grouping and regrouping like atoms, like square-dancers. But the fact was neither of us had the courage, neither of us had a strong enough wish to leave the people we were married to now. After all, Lewis gives me that lack of interest that creates the peaceful territory in which I work. I think one must admit that a lack of interest is, if nothing else, very relaxing. No sneaking, no peeking, I work in freedom. And he's proud of me at the openings of exhibitions. "Your husband's so proud of you," the other doctors' wives say wistfully as they stand about, glamorous but shy in their dull astronaut satin blouses, their accomplished puzzled eyes looking out from under their Arp-like white felt helmets, the free gallery coffee going cold in their cups. Their stockings look as if they had neatly wallowed each leg in metallic silver sugar, their shoes are of some strange American medium like a patent-leather kind of metal, like the body of a car, really, and with large square silver buckles, Pilgrim Father buckles, on the fronts. "It must be wonderful to paint," the doctors' wives say, their voices soft with regret. But maybe their regret is not only *for* Lewis' pride, but also *like* it—short-lived, assumed only for the occasion.

So Johnnie and I decided that if he cared about my painting and I cared about his film-making, and we thought we did, then we couldn't go on like this. And if we couldn't go on like this, then we couldn't go on. You see! Logic is dangerous! So we decided to give ourselves to the end of the month (that was October) to see if we'd change our minds. And we were clever about this because on November first Johnnie was due to go on a month's location in Brazil. This way we could give our separation a forced beginning. And so in the end we didn't change our minds. If he wouldn't then I wouldn't. In fact, where I had once been willing to lay myself on the line, I was now filled with the most monstrous secret pride. So October 31st was the last day for us. Hallowe'en day. And while the children were at school, Johnnie came as planned. I had been in the workroom, finishing some masks for the children, which I had promised to make as hideous as possible. Papier-mâché warts, paint-blood trickling from goitrous acrylic eyes, multicoloured raffia hair. I was carrying the masks as I ran downstairs to answer the door. For a moment I thought of putting one of the masks on, but then I could see through the glass to his stricken face (at least I thought it was stricken, I *hoped* it was stricken) and changed my mind. And he later told me that he had planned to say "Trick or treat" to me, but that he had seen my face bobbing along like a frightened flower and he too had changed his mind. But about the other, the big thing, we would not change our minds. So we would take the Lovers' Leap, but in different directions. So we would cling like strong-willed idiots to our noble decision. And so Johnnie went. And later, when the children came home from school, and I was bending flushed to help them with their costumes, I was thinking, Oh my little children, if only you could know as you come weeping home from the tragedies of recess, if only you could know that it never ends.

Hallowe'en is really the ideal children's festival. Incognito, masked like hold-up men, they go off with their opened bags that the neighbours are obliged to fill with candy and apples. Lately, though, in our city, there have been razor blades in some of the apples, some of the candies are chocolate-covered moth-balls, giving a terrible reality to all the pretence of tricks and witches. All the children have been instructed to bring home their haul so that their parents can go through it to see if it's all safe to eat. Candies are sniffed at and cracked open. Apples are drawn and quartered, and even, by those who believe terribly in the ingenuity of the wicked, made into apple sauce.

After the children had gone I sat very still on my kitchen chair. A limp rag doll stuffed with loss. Only twice the doorbell rang. The same little boy both times. Dressed up in a kind of bell-hop's or messenger's uniform. Once at the front door. Five minutes later at the back door. But our house is on a corner, he probably crossed the street, went to a few houses on the other side, then recrossed to our side and by now, in the dark and at the back, with the lighted back porch nothing more than a hanging blob of illuminated bricks, thought it was a different house. His expression, when he saw me at the back door, was one of extreme shock. I knew this little boy was not afraid of me. My bone structure may be haphazard but I'm no witch. Children usually like me, as a matter of fact, and this little boy was not afraid of me. He was only afraid of the fact that he had seen a woman exactly like me, and wearing the same clothes, and offering the same white plastic bowl of candies, only two or three houses ago. He was afraid for his own sanity. In his red suit with its double row of gold buttons, he stood for a moment, the fear flaring up in his eyes, then he turned and fled. But my fear of madness could not be run from. I went inside and sat down with it again.

The children came back, so loaded with loot they could hardly stagger in. Their masks had been pulled down and were bobbing like giant and grotesque medallions at their necks. Above them their real faces shone. And now it's two weeks since Hallowe'en and the candy supply has still not run out. Maybe the caramel creams are propagating down there in those shopping-bags. But now I've decided something. I've decided I will make a pact with myself. When the last candy is gone, I promise myself that I will face the fact that the affair is over.

Since Johnnie has gone away all the leaves have gone from the trees. A little while ago in the middle of one night I wakened to the sound of a dense rain. With the probing kick of a swimmer I hunted for Lewis in the bed, but he wasn't there. And while I was lying there, surfacing through sleep, the rain in the sky thickened and deepened. It was as if the sky I knew was only a small sky and a door in that small sky had been thrown open to a larger sky where it rained harder than any rain I'd ever known. The sound of that rain moved through my body like a blush. And when I wakened again it was morning and all the leaves had been rained from the trees, except for one high clot of them caught between two branches like a large and accidental nest. I could see up to it from my relatively low bedroom window. And the house was filled with the most uncanny light. People think of November as being the darkest month, but in our house November fills the rooms with light. In such a light I should be painting all the time.

Like I said, Lewis is a doctor. A general practitioner. The Renaissance man of the medical profession. He works with the incurably sane, all those people whose sadness goes to their joints or their bronchial tubes. It's tiring work. He often comes home tired. He used to smile shyly looking at my paintings, but the last few years he hasn't had much time even to smile shyly, he has been very busy, and the figures stand and sit unnoticed in the large workroom. Lewis is very good-looking, at parties women who are perfect strangers to me come over and tell me how lucky I am. Nobody would be apt to tell me I was lucky to have Johnnie, nobody even knew I *had* him, for one thing, but Johnnie isn't the kind of man women envy you for on sight. On the other hand, Lewis and I look mismatched, I think, therefore it is a marriage people think will last. (When all around us ideal marriages are going on the rocks, people will find their own corollaries for these troubled times.) But things are not so good with us, his highly developed bedside manner comes between us in bed. He has brought that distance so necessary to his work between us. Or maybe I'm the one who wants the distance. Maybe I'm the one who's made it so. It's very hard to tell, in a marriage, who moves away first. It's like sitting in a train station with a train bound in the opposite direction sitting next to you. When one of the trains starts moving it isn't always easy to tell which one it is. And that must be a metaphor that's been around.

"You're crazy," Lewis sometimes says to me, and when we were first married I didn't know whether this was a diagnosis or simply a friendly remark. Later I came to see that it was simply a friendly remark —because Lewis doesn't believe in madness. The people who have the grace to channel their madness into their joints and bronchioles he treats with the drugs used for treating arthritics and asthmatics, and as for the others, the ones he can't treat because they don't have symptoms, they should, according to him, just pull themselves together. I never studied painting. I studied drawing for a few years, never painting. The painting I began when I felt very uneasy when the children were small. I found that it soothed me to paint. Although sometimes it seemed both to aggravate and soothe the condition of strangeness at the same time. I sometimes felt my world pushed to a point I could hardly bear, and then I had to paint a very great deal to relieve the burden I carried in my caged-in inner eye. I don't know where these people come from, these people that I paint. I paint them in the deceptively pretty colours of the nursery. Nursery pink for the faces. Nursery blue for the eyes. Yet the faces are built up with heavy fan-shapes made in the thick paint with the palette knife, so that they seem pink and bulbous, and the eyes are almost lost in all this paint and are rather pig-like. The heads are either fair or hairless. Although sometimes under top-heavy hats which are strangely both crude and elaborate. And whether I paint them standing in subways or sitting at tea parties in deep dark gardens, they seem all to have the swayed, lulled look of people in transit. They seem to be people who are suffering, but without the heroic distinguishing marks of gauntness, deprivation, obvious anguish. They suffer, but out of a perverse integrity, I will not allow them to look poetic about it.

A few years ago I asked Lewis if he could arrange for me to make some drawings on the public wards of the hospital where he worked. He was able to fix it for me, and I spent weeks of spring afternoons there. Every Tuesday and Thursday I walked past the Emergency Department operating rooms that were small caves of light, and out onto the vast public wards. And there I sat, drawing the bed-ridden, the slowly dying, the accident cases. People, even dying people, like to be drawn. And the more mobile cases, the ones on crutches, in wheel-chairs, hobbled and wheeled around me. "Hey, Mrs. Stein . . . ! Draw me, hey Mrs. Stein?" And I did, I drew them all, drew their faces that were both stiff and loose, that had a kind of stiffly-held looseness that may have come from wishing to look incredibly strong-willed and incredibly good-natured at one and the same time. In order to counteract this self-consciousness, I sometimes drew them while they were playing cards (I learned to move quieter than any nurse) or I sat behind the East Ward TV set while they were watching it in order to catch their eyes free of that self-imposed look of distance that they seemed to think was so essential for artists' models to have. And when it worried them that I didn't always bother about representational likenesses, I told them that all good artists and all honest people know this important fact: that the truth is best told by not being too preoccupied with the telling of it. Pretty neat, that, but also true. And not an excuse for bad draughtsmanship as it might at first appear. And I told them that thing that someone—was it Picasso?—said once: "All art is lies in search of the

45

truth." And I also remember saying (I had just finished reading *Art and Reality*), that when you distort things you often make them more true, more real.

"You get a better class of reality that way," said the clever dying man in the bed by the window. A man called Dexter.

"You mean like in political cartoons?" a boy on crutches asked me, ignoring Dexter.

"It's a good example," I said.

"Not that anything any politician does ever requires distorting," said Dexter, from the taut white throne of his bed.

I remember that afternoon so clearly—all the men's ward smells—that composite of urine, grapes, cigarette ash and ointments. And when the portfolio came out it was called *Stein on Pain* and it went through a couple of reprintings. The blurb spoke of the "linear integrity" of my work. And Johnnie sat looking and looking at the drawings in a way that was excruciatingly flattering. "What do you think of the title?" I asked him, nestling in close.

"Reminds me of an English town."

"An English town! Why?"

"Oh, *you know* . . . Stoke-on-Trent . . . Stratford-on-Avon. . . ." He leaned down with a beautiful conjurer's smile, "Styne-on-Payne."

After that I called it my English Town portfolio, which puzzled everybody.

But about Lewis and his profession: there is even another way they have been helpful to me in my work. In giving names to the drawings and canvases, for instance. A girl dancing I titled "Symphisis Pubis" and this girl caused one critic to cite "witty cubistic echoes" in my work. The medico-organic names must have been what inspired one of the gallery owners to describe my technique as "abstract organic neo-classicism rooted in glorification of the body." This pleased me, for a while I was even able to say it very

46

fast like a tongue-twister, now I have to think carefully to recall how it went. And what's more to figure out exactly what it means. I don't do many physiological things though. In fact I'm not good at them, and never was, even when I was younger and under the mistaken impression that they were the thing to do. I prefer my strange people. Sometimes they are sitting in subways, as I said, sometimes in buses, sometimes in gardens, sometimes in men's clubs where the furniture is upholstered in black leather (I have a fetish about painting black leather) and the Persian rugs look, in the paintings, like magnificent organizations of stains.

Johnnie told me once that he came to care a great deal for the disturbed children he filmed. And he also told me that my portfolio of hospital drawings had given him an idea for a short movie. He said he was thinking of filming it from a hospital bed, as if he was paralyzed or helpless, so that the camera would be always at pillow-level—would take in the tight bellies of nurses, the giant shaking of thermometers, the injections that move in for the kill that cures. Only when the bed was cranked up (and you would hear the cranks as the image jumped), only then, at the very end of the film, would you finally see faces.

I have been lying here in the bed for some time. When we came home with the groceries, the children and I, I remembered the pact I had made with myself to face the facts about Johnnie. And I stood under the dull hall light, a tall tired woman slowly pulling off gloves, finger by leather finger. Good tobacco-coloured gloves they are, with little portholes for the knuckles. I stuffed them, port-holes and all, into my dark coat pocket. After that, I felt the shopping bags that were in the hall closet to try to gauge how the Hallowe'en supply was holding out, how many days I might have before the deadline of the last caramel cream. There were still quite a few in each of the bags.

If each child ate its share at the rate of three candies a day, I figured I'd still have about ten days' grace. Then just before I sent them up to bed I heard the three of them out in the hall closet. Ferreting. "Don't eat too many of those candies, now!" I yelled. "You know they're not good for your teeth!" Just to help myself along a little.

But after I'd got them all settled in and was getting ready for bed myself, I started worrying. Sometimes I think I was too possessive, that he somehow made the break-up appear to be something we both needed —for our work and even for our feeling about each other. I get very frightened when I have these thoughts. I can't bear that it should be like that. Or like anything else either. I can't bear that it should be over. I would like the possibility of our being together to be somehow protected. That's what I started to think. And of course the possibility always *is* there. If I phoned him when he came back from Brazil and said, "I can't stand this any more," I expect we could pick up where we left off. But still the possibility wasn't strong enough. I felt I had to do something to seal its strength. "You get a better class of reality that way," I remembered Dexter pronouncing from the white heights of his death-bed. And from my helpless position on my own bed all I could see from pillow-level was how the avenidas of São Paulo, Brazil, would be filled with photogenic dark girls, their white blouses sluiced by sun.

It's strange: for almost ten years—ever since I starting painting—I've been making patterns out of reality. Now I find myself wanting to make reality out of patterns. Because of this, I'm glad Lewis is out of town. If he had seen me perhaps he would have begun at last to believe in madness. I put the caftan on (the one that Johnnie had bought for me once in Cairo). I searched in my jewelry drawer for the little snap-jawed box. It was a mess in the jewelry drawer. Some black chiffon scarves had got mixed up with the brooches and beads and bracelets and rings. The costume jewelry shone out with muted sparkle through the purdah of black chiffon. It was like having a crowd of Mohammedan women down in there. I found the snap-jawed box and lifted it out. And after blindly seeking through all the tangle at the bottom, after walking my bead-reined fingers along the ocean floor of my drawer, I also found its key. The key I put into my pyjama pocket. The snap-jawed box I held to what bosom I have and I moved quickly, barefoot, down the dark stairs. When I got to the bottom I didn't bother to turn on the light. I knelt in the dark of the hall closet and put my hand into the mouth of the first shopping bag. I lifted one candy up from it and put it into my pyjama pocket. Everything was businesslike as a dream. Then I went into the mouth of the second bag and got another candy for my pocket. And the same with the third. Then I went out to the kitchen and turned on the big cold kitchen light. I hitched the caftan up and took the three candies out of my pocket and put them on the counter. Then with the key I opened the snap-jawed box. On its miniature velvet platform I placed the three candies. One caramel cream. Two square toffees. Three jewels. I closed the box. Locked it. Now the candies would never be completely gone. Possibility would be locked in there forever. There remained only the problem of what to do with the key. Outside the ground was already frozen so I couldn't go out and dig a hole to put it in. The garbage did not seem safe, someone might retrieve it. I thought of throwing it into the fireplace, but it occurred to me that it might not melt in the heat and might later be found in the ashes. I decided finally on the plumbing. I would flush it down the toilet. But I would have to wrap it in something to give it some volume. I went to one of the kitchen cupboards and took out a large paper napkin. Carefully I wrapped the

49

key in it. I even scotch-taped the ends of this small strange parcel, then carried it with me to the downstairs toilet. I threw it into the bowl and pressed the flush. At once it was mercifully rushed from view. I washed my hands, went back to the kitchen to get the box, turned out the light, then climbed in the darkness up to my bedroom. In the dark of my room I dropped the snap-jawed box into the deep jewelry drawer which I then closed.

Now I'm back in the bed. But a frightening possibility has occurred to me. If I can believe I can control the future, maybe I am also obliged to believe I can control the past. And if I can control the past it's possible that I have invented everything that I *say* has happened. After all, I can almost hear you cry, "The genre is familiar—although it's often distinguished by a redeeming madness; stream of consciousness of an intelligent housewife (written, perhaps, by a French novelist). Furthermore, it's also somewhat overwrought and self-conscious, in spite of its good parts. Furthermore," I can hear you add, "it's not as moving as it should be." But how can anyone decide for you how moving your own life should be? And how did such a familiar genre (lovers, meetings, partings, longings) lead into this strange swamp? Why does Johnnie make films, for instance? Because it's simply convenient? A graphic way of breaking the ego boundaries in a cinematic dissolve? And why am I a painter? So that I can say, "The figures in my paintings waited for me to change or finish them. And our relationship also waited. Waited for us to change or finish it." Two kinds of images: images on film, images on canvas. Images that are believed to be real, images that are believed to be invented. *But who knows what's real? Who knows what's invented? Am* I a painter? *Does* Johnnie make films? I can even ask myself the two most terrifying questions of all, in ascending order of terror, since the second question lives like a challenging embryo in the innards of the first. . . . *Did any of this really happen? Do we exist?*

But I must forget all this and emphasize the positive. I can imagine, for instance, that the little box with possibility locked in it is my survival kit, and that the whole point of this survival kit is that there is no key. On that its value rests. Suddenly, I feel strangely safe, and I know I soon will sleep.

SUMMER MOURNINGS, 1959

Indignation made them efficient. They were bending toward each other across the bed, in grim unison straining the sheets tight over the corners. It was a big bed, conceived (in happier days) for two, but large enough for a whole family—now their mother slept in it alone. And she was impossible, they said, pounding the pillows plump. She was irresponsible. She was behaving like a child. They asked each other how long it had been going on anyway, their being left with all the housework every morning, a question which of course they knew the answer to, but which gave them comfort, like a litany. They had got out of school only two weeks before, prepared to help in the antique shop (which she was magnificent about, they had to admit that; and admitting it made them aware that it was quite possible for them to be angry and still be *fair*, whereas *she* was always very *un*fair when she was cross, and they were reminded that this was yet another sphere where they were outstripping her, as what Chrissie called the "parent-child roles" became more and more reversed). And it wasn't as if they minded doing their share, they said—they didn't. It had all been agreed on in advance that they were to work in the shop in the afternoons, every day from one till six, and they didn't mind, but to work all the mornings too, to not have any time off, while all over Walkerton the doctors' daughters, the pharmacist's daughters, the daughters of the men who owned the men's-wear stores on Queen Street were climbing out of bed and into bikinis. We'll never get tanned, they said sadly, looking at the socially unacceptable whites of their arms. Chrissie rotated hers in the light; "Condemned bah the collah of mah skin" she said, and looking up from their laughter, their eyes naturally sought the windows, which showed them the sun shining unfairly down on the world outside. It glanced off the spiral of the Catholic cathedral and it undoubtedly shone down on their mother also, as with a simulated air of rush she went from the electrician's to the post-office to the supermarket.

And yet it went on. Every morning they would watch the ritual of their mother in flight before the morning's work was about to begin. They would exchange resigned glances, glances of gloomy prediction confirmed. Katie, though, always seemed completely unaware of the exchange of looks, working her feet into her sandals while she was still eating her toast, rising with coffee-cup in hand to collect her purse, her cardigan, her car keys, letting the snatching of food—the selflessness of refusing to sit down and give herself a proper breakfast—give a sense of urgency to what was, after all, only another unnecessary trip downtown. It was pathetic, they reassured each other, really pathetic, to watch her go through the whole pretence of genuinely having something to do, and Anne had a sudden clear recollection of her, her pretty mother, her thick fair hair done into a smooth fat French twist, haunches lowered, her flowered sun-dress dipping to a full circle around her, extricating from one of the dim kitchen cupboards an old electric kettle which she was telling them had to be taken to the electrician's for repairs; other mornings, other relics-in-need-of-repair would materialize: if not, the car could always be depended on to have something wrong with it, or there would be someone sick to be visited, or she would need to pick up groceries—groceries which, they would both agree, could much more easily have been got by phone. It was flattering to be relied on, they decided, but it could so easily lead to being exploited; the line between the two was very thin.

Once the bed was made, its broad white planes ruled the room. The scattered untidiness of tables and bureaux receded, shored against the walls in a kind of decorativeness. They began dropping clothes into drawers and reunited pairs of shoes into the pockets of plastic shoe-bags, sighing with the deep regularity of people being x-rayed. The big bureau was a mess—a nylon stocking had got caught on the bristles of a hairbrush, a white glove lay on the one small area of dresser where face-powder had previously been spilled, as if Katie's possessions had conspired to make as much trouble for them as possible. Chrissie picked up the glove and beat it smartly against her Bermuda shorts, but the stain remained.

"Should we wash it, I wonder—?" Anne asked.

"Like hell we should!" Chrissie said, and she threw it down on the bed so that when Katie came in she would see it—and be humbled by it. Then they went through the tangle of jewelry on the dresser. Occasionally one of them would extricate a single piece, and holding it to her, to her throat, to her ear, to an imaginary lapel, would go to the mirror, as if to have a question answered. They did that with her clothes too, solemnly holding dresses and blouses to their young fronts before they committed them to the closet.

"Sentenced to hang," Chrissie would say each time she picked up a crumpled piece of clothing from one of the chairs, "Sentenced to hang," and they would both roar with laughter, and she would hold it to her in front of the mirror and then fit it onto a hanger.

"I wish she would lend me this sometime," Anne

said, holding a pleated cocktail dress to waist and shoulder.

"Fat chance," Chrissie said, which wasn't quite correct. Katie was dangerously good at lending them things. Several times a year, too, she pruned her wardrobe of what was stained in the armpits or fallen in the hem, and gave the girls first choice before the pile was given to the cleaning-woman. Chrissie usually found excuses for not accepting these things, knowing their acceptance forfeited her chances of getting anything new, but Anne often took them, sometimes even with gratitude, which to Chrissie seemed pure lunacy.

"Well, I see Mawmaw has had her bawth," said Chrissie when they came into the bathroom. Katie's soap, rosy and slippery, lay swaddled in a wet washcloth in the bottom of the tub. Chrissie grunted down to fetch it and gave a few token swipes to the sides of the tub while Anne straightened out the towels. At last, they were finished, at long and beautiful last. They went to the mirror, lifted their hair from their damp necks and wiped themselves lavishly with Katie's cologne. "Be feminine," Katie would often exhort them. "Men like women to. . . ." This was an opener they supplied their own endings to. "Men like women to be *feminine*," was the way it ran with Katie, but they altered it to "Men like women to change their panties four times a day," or "Men like women to make farts that contain a distinctive bouquet, the aroma of wild-flowers—." Their fingers would wipe the sweat from their arm-pits and then move up to wipe the tears from their laughing eyes. They were aware themselves of the way they took a certain adolescent satisfaction in dealing democratically with their body secretions. Once in the den, free of Katie's room and Katie's arsenal, they helped themselves each to a cigarette, threw themselves down into chairs and kicked off their sandals.

Over their cigarettes, though, their eyes were listening, for it was impossible to assess from her departing mood what her home-coming mood would be. She was never very explicit when she went off in the mornings. "Clear up a bit, darlings!" she would call gaily from the front doorway, not wanting, in her guilt about going, and her eagerness to be gone, to actually list the things that needed to be done. Then the remarkable romanesque door with the built-in fan-light (which she had been lucky enough to salvage from an old house in Woodstock and which she had then had built into the facade of their own house) would open, throwing its fan of inverted pyramids of light briefly across the floor. Almost at once, this pattern would be snatched back into place as the door was slammed to, and a moment later they would hear her start the car and pull off. And no matter how much they resented her going, her leaving all the work to them, the moment of her leaving was one of the most intense relief, as if the exhaling of a gigantic sigh suffused the house, so that they prolonged the Sunday feeling with extra cups of coffee and cigarettes, postponing as long as possible the rush, which kept growing of course, in a kind of perverse ratio to its postponement. The times that she had bad days downtown though, and came back with her eyes tired and her arms weighted with groceries, they would discover that their jobs had been multiplying while she was away, had become more explicit, so that she was alarmed that they had not realized that such and such was to be done, *surely they could have seen that for themselves*! It got so that they soon learned to for they were both afraid of her anger—of the intense, bitter silence which could, if necessary, be maintained for days, of a vacant hostile look in her eyes, close to madness.

"Mummie," they would plead (being reduced to calling her Mummie, even though for years they had called her Katie), "Mummie," they would plead,

"Mummie, will you have some coffee?" and there would only be that deliberately uncomprehending stare, striking terror in them.

"Mummie," they would say, "Mummie, we are leaving for school now, okay?" There would be no indication that she had heard, and they would go off, relieved to be gone, but frightened of leaving her alone too, wondering what she might do to herself, so that their whole day at school would be distinguished by nervous mistakes and catastrophic inattention. And sometimes, with a kind of regal coldness, Katie would take to her bed and sit up against three pillows—a fair, fine-boned doll with burning polar empty eyes. Since she was never sick, her taking to her bed like this seemed an act of the most melodramatic revenge, and on these occasions all her memories would be grievances and her daughters would minister to her with both anxiety and contempt, bringing her white bowls filled with pale orange smudged tomato soup, or fresh fruit that carried a truant air of summer into the hot dead closed room. Ordinarily she would not speak to them (except to tell them how selfish they were or to lament her own failure as a mother; they knew they were expected to deny the second lament but that it would be madness to try to deny the first); sometimes she would pick a fight with one of them, usually Anne, and would thrash out of bed and start screaming and crying threats; sometimes she would lie on the floor, on her back, and there would be an imperious rain of heels on the floor-boards. Sometimes she would lunge at the windows and threaten to throw herself out. Once, when she had run to a window and was struggling, weeping and gasping, with the fastening, Anne, terrified, had cried, "Alright, if you feel that way, I'm going to call a doctor!" and had reached for the phone. Katie had wheeled around at once, and had lept across the room and had pounced on the phone like a panther taking possession of a mouse. "*Don't you dare interfere with my life!*" she had cried, "*Keep away from that phone!*" From panther to lioness, from black rage to golden fury. Her daughters had fled from the room, their hearts beating at locketpoint inside their frightened constricted throats. At such times it did not seem to Anne that she was a Canadian, living in Canada. Her mother's rages and silences seemed to belong to a darker, more dramatic country, to a more mythic time. Lifting her eyes from her mother's face, she would be amazed to see, through the window, the pink ranch-style houses that sat on the bright green hillside next to their boundary line, would be amazed to see, below them, the long concessions that ran like grass canals all the way down to the alder-banked river. Always, though, a few days after these terrors, Katie would be fine, she would be laughing, full of plans, she would want to be their friend. Flanked by her two tall pale daughters, she would pose for tourists' photographs in the back orchard where shadows like shoe-horns and arrowheads and berries would spot their shoulders and their summer dresses. "I don't know what I'd do without these two," she'd say with a sunny smile, squeezing her daughters' waists to her own; as if the three of them made up some kind of human accordion, and Chrissie and Anne would be charmed, like her, like the tourists, like the camera, into believing totally in the moment's mirage of family contentment and unity. In the long run, though, only Chrissie was seduced; Chrissie accepted Katie's overtures of friendship the way Anne accepted Katie's clothes, sometimes even with gratitude, which to Anne seemed pure lunacy. But the bad episodes were always worst for Anne, who felt herself to be the awful and only cause of her mother's anger; Chrissie was more objective and often rationalized it in simple terms, sometimes even in single words, like "Daddy" before

the menopause, and after the menopause, "menopause."
And they never told anyone anything about what went
on at home. No-one would believe them for one thing,
and for another, Katie would kill them if they did.

Both girls were very fond of a kind of psychological
speculation ("gossip, really, but on a higher plane"), and
sitting with their eyes listening over their cigarettes,
they analyzed Katie. And although they knew nothing
about the circular ironies that fence in the adult lives of
those who have been voluptuous girl children, they
were fond of saying that she had the body of a sex
queen and the mind of a missionary. They were not
misled by the fact that she was fond of talking to them
about sex, which she told them she was good at,
because the more she tried to inform them, the more
firmly they became convinced of her embarrassing and
pathetic innocence. As for her daily forays downtown,
they decided that it was not so much what she was
escaping *from* (they, after all, took care of that), as what
she was escaping *to*; it was apparent to them that her
trips downtown gave her back herself. They lamented
that none of the other kids had mothers like *her*, other
kids they knew didn't even want to *talk* about their
mothers, they were bored by their mothers, but
Chrissie and Anne talked about Katie almost
continuously; in their minds she was oppressor,
specimen, curiosity, star. And they imagined her, their
morning's oppressor and star, downtown, buoyed up
by the glances of the men, preening herself in her mind.
They knew that finally, at morning's end, her arms
loaded with bounty from the A & P (where the cashier
was always so cheerful and kind), she would return
home, rehabilitated.

Anne, seated near the window, was the first to hear
the warning sound of the car as it hit the gravel drive-

way. She stubbed her cigarette on the bottom of her sandal and carried it into the toilet where she dropped it into the flush. After she had flushed it away, she went to the sink, turned the tap on full force and drank from it open-mouthed.

"There!" she said, wiping her mouth with the back of her hand, "I should be in some kind of espionage work!"

"Well," said Chrissie languidly, "you've certainly destroyed the evidence."

She let the smoke drift out of her mouth. Downstairs, the door slammed. They walked across the upstairs hallway.

"You look like a train," Anne said in her warning way. Chrissie blew out more smoke—"*Whoooooo Whoooooo*," she sang in a little girl's voice, "*Whoooooo Whoooooo, I'm a twain, I'm a twain!*" Anne silenced her out of the tail of one of her pale frightened eyes, and they began to descend the stairs, as suddenly-solemn as bridesmaids.

Chrissie relieved Katie of her parcels at the bottom of the stairway and held her cigarette out at a ridiculous and obvious angle as she carried the groceries into the kitchen. Katie, adjusting to the inside dark after the sun-and-mica brilliance of outside, noticed only two things: that Chrissie was the one who was being helpful and that Anne was looking guilty about something. She spoke sharply to Anne once, resting her hand fondly on Chrissie's shoulder while doing so, and Anne, who had at first admired Chrissie's aplomb, now began to resent it. The resentment stayed with her all day, and although she frequently reminded herself that it was not Chrissie who had been at fault, but she herself who had been underhanded, she could not rid herself of the notion that in some subtle but savage way she had been compromised.

At lunch that day, Chrissie went to work on Katie

about the movie. One that she had wanted to see for ages was, wonder of wonders, now at the Rialto, and she was determined to go. The checkered table-cloth might have been a chessboard, so correctly did she anticipate and counter her mother's objections across it. Anne sat watching her with a mixture of skepticism and hope, absently blowing on her now-cold soup each time she spooned it up. She wished her luck, she wanted to go too, but she didn't need to worry, she told herself, Chrissie could get them anything. She thought of the times Chrissie had been sent out to buy things for Katie at the drug store, of how she would come back laden with extra things, with bath-oil, with the latest copy of *Mademoiselle*, and say, "For you, Katie dear, presents," and later spike her own bath with the oil and read the magazine herself, which was what she had intended to do all along. Katie never failed to be touched and delighted with these impromptu gifts, and it was very unlikely that it ever occurred to her that she had paid for them herself. The thought that Katie, who could be as coldly suspicious as any medieval queen, should be such a trusting baby with Chrissie, filled Anne with a dull anger, an anger that left a tarnished taste in her mouth and made her move in a way that was clumsy and dumb.

"Thank you, dear, but I don't think I could swing it tonight," Katie was saying to Chrissie, for that was how Chrissie had approached it of course, that this was a film that Katie, in particular, would enjoy. "But you two go, why don't you?" she asked unexpectedly.

"But it's sad you can't come," Chrissie said in a voice Anne thought too quickly soothing to be sincere. Chrissie reached over and patted her mother's arm.

"Are you really sure you couldn't make it?"

"No, Chrissie dear, no, I can't," she said, flattered, "I really must invite the Martins in for drinks."

Usually the three of them went everywhere together, especially at night, because Katie hated to go out (or stay in) alone. Their father was a geologist and while he was away on field-trips, which was often, Katie required the girls' protection. But it was not to be *called* protection, ever, it was to be called "companionship."

In the antique shop it seemed as if the afternoon would never end. And it was hot. There was a run on wooden ladles and milk glass, both inexpensive. But at last it looked as if they could soon close. They were running, as they so often did, overtime. Katie had got involved with some people from Massachusetts. Obviously she hoped they would soon go, but was so afraid they would sense her eagerness that each time they seemed on the point of their crest-fallen departure, she detained them with yet another print, yet another auction story. People often felt very possessive with Katie. It was not only—as the woman from Massachusetts had just said—that she was "such a little doll," it was also that people soon sensed that she depended on them for love and admiration, that she was renewed by being needed, that kindly people were necessary to her existence and so had a kind of claim on her. Now her sentences were rushed and flurried, as if flushed up like startled birds from the undergrowth of memory, while her upper mind went on dealing with its everyday problems, phone calls she should make, letters she should write. At last they were allowed to go. She shut her eyes against their sad, broad backs (real tourists' backs, suspendered with camera straps), and quietly closed the door. "At last," she said. Then they linked arms, the three of them, and with heads bowed and laughing, they pounded up the formal circular stairway, breathless to their supper.

After they had done the supper dishes, the girls put on their high-school blazers and left the house. They had passed through the shadow of the last tree that heralded the upward sweep of driveway before they began to talk. By the time they reached the highway on the outskirts of the town, they were arguing.

"You *use* people," Anne was saying.

"And *you don't*, I suppose."

"I hope I don't."

"Well, you do, honey, you do, in your own rather sinister way you do, just as much as I do."

"So you admit it then?"

"Admit what?"

"That you use people."

Chrissie sighed. "Everybody uses people. But go ahead, tell me how I do, obviously you're dying to."

Anne said: "The way you're always railroading Mother into buying you new clothes, for instance."

"Well, why not? I like nice clothes, and she can afford it, can't she? Lord knows, she buys herself enough of them. Besides, I *do* get invited out occasionally"—she looked at Anne a full moment here—"I like to have something half-decent to wear. You don't even live in this century, that's what's the matter with you, you think you don't even have to try in life, you think you just have to sit there, blushing and demure, and some handsome colonial officer will arrive one day at the door, be suh-wept by your bew-tee and carry you off. Life isn't like that, life isn't like something out of *Jane Eyre*!"

"What's wrong with Jane Eyre?"

"There's nothing wrong with Jane Eyre, for crying out loud, or with Jane Austen! But, good God, things have been written since then! And life isn't all books either."

Anne's smile broke shyly over protruding teeth. Chrissie looked at her sister critically. It seemed to her that Anne was both vague and earnest, that Anne drove her into these earnest, dumb, meaningless conversations, that Anne was commonplace and was making her commonplace too.

"You're not loyal, either," Anne said, making her feel suddenly uneasy.

"Like when?" Chrissie asked her.

"To Daddy, for instance."

"But I've never even pretended to particularly like Daddy. I know *you* think he's a *saint* or something, that doesn't mean *I* have to like him."

"You aren't loyal to Katie, either, the way you were talking about her this morning."

"Ha!" snorted Chrissie, in a loud deductive voice, "Ha!" She turned her shrewd gaze on Anne, letting it rove all over her face. "Don't be a little snot, Anne," she said in a dangerous quiet voice, "if I recollect correctly, you enjoyed that conversation quite a bit yourself."

"But I've never even pretended to particularly like Katie," Anne said, throwing it back. They were both able to see the humour of this and to laugh shakily.

"Touché," said Chrissie.

And "Alright," said Chrissie later, in a voice that was harsh and belligerent but also puzzled, "Alright, I'm not particularly loyal. I'm more objective, really. Objective enough to admit I'm not loyal anyway."

Then she said, "And *you* use people too."

Anne genuinely wondered how. "How?" she asked.

"*How*!—Alright, answer me this: quite frankly now, if we went down to the swimming pool every day like the other kids, you wouldn't have much fun, would you? I mean, socially, you aren't exactly in demand—well, *are you*? So isn't it quite convenient if you can blame it all on Mother who never lets you out anywhere? Isn't it?"

"If you think I like staying home working all the time, you're crazy."

"I didn't say you liked the *work*," Chrissie said. I just said it was *convenient*. It's like the way you're always

64

accepting Mother's old clothes and then saying that that's why nobody asks you to the school dances. I'm not saying Mother doesn't have her faults, but I'm not saying you're perfect either."

Anne had a sudden intuitive fear of seeing the movie. It would be full of upsetting thoughts, she knew it. All very well for Chrissie, who liked to think upsetting thoughts, she even pretended that she liked to think them about herself. I don't want to see, Anne thought, alarmed. I don't want to understand. But the Rialto was already in sight, on Pond Street, filling in the gap at the end of Manor Avenue. They could see the title mounted on the marquee. Lights were running on a track around the title, automated, organic—like ticker-tape, like sap. Chrissie was pondering the slip-up that had permitted a good film to be featured, smiling happily to herself, thinking how disappointed everyone was going to be.

Old Lou was out watering her garden. "Hello, girls!" she called. "Going to the pictures?"

"Yes!" they called back, "Some Swedish thing!"

"Ah," she called sagely, "Sounds interesting! How's your mother?"

"Fine!" their voices floated back over the hedges, weakening with distance, "Fine!"

Liddy was edging out through the screen door with a cumbersome pan of heavy swinging water. "Who was that?" she said.

"The MacLean girls, going to the Rialto."

"Pretty girl, that Chrissie," said Liddy. "Bright too, they say. Hear she's getting a scholarship to go to the collitch." She was at the sunken end of the verandah, slaking the thirst of the delphiniums with dirty dishwater.

"I always liked Anne, myself," said Lou.

"Anne!" cried Liddy. "Well, I can't think why. Looks just like her Auntie Fran. Same teeth and everything."

Lou didn't answer. The two MacLean girls in their matching blazers made her think of herself and Liddy, of how they had matching dowager humps on their backs, and the same fat ankles. When they had been younger they had prided themselves on their differences, but gradually time and flesh and failing memory had equalized them, it was now quite common for people to confuse one with the other. Once Liddy had gone to bed though, Lou shone in the dark garden. Aiming streams of water cold as ether into the warm earth. When she got tired from the watering she sat down on the grass to rest. All day she had felt a strange congestion around her heart—as if a jungle was growing in her chest. She felt an overwhelming need to close her eyes, but before she would allow herself to do so she wanted to take one last look at the flocks of leaves, black against a sky that was going from aquamarine to milk.

When the girls came down to breakfast next morning, Katie was there already. When she saw them, she sighed. "Lou Morrison died last night," she said. "Old Lou?" they asked, incredulous. "But we saw her!" they protested. "Just last night! In her garden! She looked fine!"

"Well, she's dead," Katie said, gathering to her the paraphernalia of consolation: the fresh-cut flowers, the sponge-cake wrapped in tin foil, the self-help book which she was shortly to press into Liddy's hand.

"And 70 isn't old," she said. "Not nowadays." She looked upset. "Not with the advances of medical science," she said. She left the room and went out to comb her hair in front of the hall mirror.

"What did she die of?" Anne called out from the kitchen. "Was it just old age?"

"No!" she shouted back. "No!"

"What, then?"

"Heart failure!"

66

Because her voice seemed to reach them from a distance, they were shocked when she appeared in the kitchen doorway, an apparition, startling them. She seemed to have lost at least twenty pounds since yesterday, but she was always like that, pinched and drawn for funerals, robust for weddings and christenings. An emotional chameleon, she adapted to occasions, not to people, and of all occasions, the funeral came closest to being her natural habitat.

"I'm ready to go now," she announced, in a voice that managed to be both woebegone and heroic.

Alright Mother, they said, Fine Mother, and Are you sure you're alright? "I'm alright," she said, and she went down the hall to the mirror again and began fitting on her hat. It was a black velvet skull cap with a squat black velvet stem. Chrissie had once said that it looked like the lid of a Hallowe'en pumpkin. Fitting it onto her head, Katie took tender cognizance of her stricken reflection.

A harsh burst of laughter came from the kitchen.

They're laughing at me, she thought. They often laugh at me.

She took off her shoes then, and carrying them in one hand, she crept down the hallway. When she got to the kitchen, she stood in the doorway, perfectly still, watching them. They were talking and laughing. She waited for several moments, their backs were turned toward her. Her hand, with the shoes hanging from it, was sweating. With her free hand, she supported herself against the door frame. Then,

"Have you no respect for the dead?" she said.

They turned around, alarmed. She had this incredible talent for making their blood run cold. They did not know what to say.

"You are very selfish," she told them. "I have tried to teach you to think of others, but I have failed."

She put her shoes on then and left the kitchen, walking sharply down the hall.

"I want the kitchen cleared up completely when I get home!" she shouted.

"Clean the oven too, and the bedrooms! And peel the vegetables for supper!"

"*How I spent my summer vacation*," said Chrissie, in an accurate imitation of Ruth Ann Hodges, the teacher's pet at school, reading her prize-winning essay at the beginning of September term. And she raised her eyes to Heaven, for strength.

They gave a brief grim snort of laughter each.

The trouble is, Chrissie was thinking, *the trouble is that I am too intelligent. I am assailed by boredom. Everything is so typical. The events. The conversations. This town. Even the name Ruth Ann Hodges is, though real, heartrendingly typical. It's all very boring and bad for me.* She stared out the window. The leaves on the trees looked like shiny green vinyl. The flowers in the flowerbeds all looked like imitations.

Anne's world was too frightening to be boring. Terror kept it fresh. She was always braced, waiting, and it seemed to her that she never had to wait long.

"Anne!" Katie shouted, on cue, her voice like the rapping of knuckles, "Put the laundry through the washer and iron the blouses!"

There was no longer the uncertainty of guilt in her voice, her voice was sure, and when she left the house she slammed the door behind her.

"Oh well, we'll probably be like that someday ourselves," said Chrissie.

Anne gave her sister a cool look. She could suddenly see into Chrissie, could see her shrewdness, could see how she was banking on escaping by having visualized the possibility that she would not escape, was banking, with a certain smugness, on a crafty humility. Anne's cool look hardened. "I'll never be like Mother," she said.

"Oh blah!" said Chrissie, over the rapid jerky drying of knives and forks.

68

They were both looking out the window as they washed and dried. They could see how the car, a small grey twinkling loaf of metal, lost the star of sun on its hood, could see the star extinguished by the living green of foliage as the car dipped to a shaded patch of driveway. There was a suspension in the room, then, as if they had stopped breathing. They felt either very old or very young—anything but their own ages, in any country but their own. Then the car turned out onto the highway and shot toward the town and they began to breathe again. But as they breathed they sighed. A death is a better excuse than an electric kettle for getting out of the house, and they were beginning to realize that from now until the funeral was over, at least, they would have their work cut out for them.

MORE LIKE BIRDS
THAN BIRDS

Timmie was sick during the first big snowstorm of the Ottawa winter and after it was over, and he was better, I put him into his navy blue nylon snowsuit (the one that gives him the high wasp-waist) and we went for a walk out into the new world. Behind us, at home, on the nurse-white tiles of his bedroom floor, we had left, standing in an oval of sunlight, his brown glass bottle of purple cough medicine, the dun-coloured humidifier and the measuring spoons splayed out into a small fan of diminishing circles. For those who like metaphors, *there* is a metaphor—a life, a smaller life, a half-life, a third of a life, a quarter. Now, walking, I hoped Timmie wouldn't talk too much; my head ached. If I moved it too suddenly, the columns of soreness wobbled, jiggling the whole edifice of pain. And he didn't, he was caught up in some kind of heroic fantasy, and with aboriginal yells and grunts he plunged a long dagger-twig over and over again into the snow-ploughed flanks of snow. We were more or less at peace. We moved in our own spheres.

When we came out onto Charlotte Street, we saw that convoys of trucks were moving out of the city. On their cabs were the letters

J. P. LACROIX AND SONS
CARTAGE
TOPSOIL AND SAND

They were filled with snow. And in the first park we came to, only the top green slat of each park-bench rose above the white. And in the open reaches, the snow had been laminated by the wind. And inland, away from the parks and the river, on the hardened snow of the sidewalks, city workmen, wearing orange canvas vests, were carrying shovels in the crooks of their arms, looking medieval, seeding the white sidewalks with sand. In the second park we came to, a grander park below the Russian Embassy, the cherubs holding up the fountain had snow up past their podium right up to their fat stone ankles; and the large gar-landed plate, where the fountain played in summer, carried, because of its protective canvas tent, a perfect pyramid of white. We walked down a narrow opening with high snow walls until we came to what at first looked like a mirage: someone had excavated an entire city park-bench. There it sat, a prosaic and surprising shrine, surrounded on three sides by high slabs of white. We sat on it.

But after a time, Timmie got tired of swinging his feet, and climbed back toward the fountain, probably to do battle with the cherubs. I could see him, or at least his red hat, once he had reached that height—a dancing anchor on the outer edge of the field of my attention. I felt glad we had come. I even felt glad we had come together. Sitting there on that first discovered artifact of that other era, summer, I saw Timmie as both limitation and revelation; there is something, I thought, about being with little children at times when you so much don't want to be with them, that jacks your perceptions up, that cracks open your old way of thinking. And archaic as it sounds, you almost have to be a mother (being a father doesn't count, unless you are a father like my father—a father we called to in the night, when we were sick or frightened); you also have to be starved for sleep, and you have to wish very much to be alone. It also helps if you've just nursed the child, and if he's been cranky, and if, during the last 24 hours, you've sometimes hated him—preferably intensely. If you are entirely by yourself, you are sometimes disoriented by the newness, the strangeness, the significance of it, but when you are with a child, you are fiercely fighting for the right to think your own thoughts; and then you do think them, and you think them fast, wholesale, entire, against the absolute certainty that you will be interrupted again and again. Sometimes it's a good way to have to think. And so I thought fast, wholesale, entire, these thoughts:

Leave Karl.

Don't.

Leave Karl.

Don't.

In winter, there are no daisies to dismember in the search for answers. Well. Begin anyway. He's a good father. Better than he used to be. He washes their hair. He's taught them to skate. He's also a fault-finder. But then I'm untidy. He's also a rational man. But then I tend to be emotional. Maybe I need his everyday oppressions. Maybe I *like* it up against the wall. Anyway, I can't imagine making the break. And meanwhile, back at the domestic heart of things, in the kitchen, I cut out calls-to-arms and autobiographical fragments from the works of women writers, and clippings about actresses and painters who've taken off somewhere, with three children and a panel truck and, after much struggle and pain, have found success, Nirvana, equilibrium, peace . . . and like a squirrel I hoard them, these clippings, bury them in my files . . . *against the day . . . when I too . . . will . . . .* Liz (friend, mentor) says, women must support women. Women must help women to move on, up, out, away. Wherever. *True.* But what if you can't? You can't legislate a leap of faith. Maybe you find freedom at the core of the oppression. *Maybe I am one of those.* Oh God, Liz would say, then you really do have a problem.

Or maybe not. Sometimes Liz gets as confused as I do.

If we go our separate ways, Karl and I both want the children.

Timmie came down the walk, his dagger-twig turned into a cane.

An old man now, back from the wars. And I thought: the fact that your child hates to see you thinking your own thoughts gives you the illusion that your own thoughts are somehow subversive. It's a pleasant illusion. It may even be real. And then because the child has, in the most curious and involuted way, been a catalyst (even if only a catalyst in the creation of an illusion), you feel warmly toward him. And then the child, atoning for a time when you did not feel so warmly, does some beautiful, redeeming thing— something that has to do with a new way of looking at the world.

I thought of: the firm manufactured-rubber look of the lips of dolphins; the face of a certain kind of owl—like a cross-section of withered apple; that most efficient of fishes, the man-eating piranha, a whole universe printed on its shimmering flesh, a whole golden galaxy of stars; all appearing in an animal encyclopedia belonging to my sons.

With Timmie, what looked like the redeeming thing happened as we were walking home, back through the first park. We passed Nesrallah's Grocery; we crossed to the old armouries. The old armouries were burnt sienna brick, and in the fall the twin trees at the back, park-side, had had wine-coloured leaves. Now the sky was a cold, solid, calendar-coloured orange and the apartment blocks of lights looked chartreuse against it. There were no people in the park, only . . .

73

"Birds!" cried Timmie, suddenly, happily, pointing to a large tree in the middle of that great white free space enclosed by a courtyard of traffic, of city life, of black, of lights.

When we got closer to this tree we saw that the flock beneath it were not birds (that was only an illusion), they were old curled leaves that had fallen after the recent storm. There were about forty of them. They were more like birds than birds, and they were feeding themselves on snow.

MAGICIANS

He was showing her his recent past, slide after slide of it. She held small views of western streets and Rocky Mountains and Pacific Ocean up to the kitchen window's light. These were from his last trip. Now he was off once more, and would soon be bringing back the *east coast* for her to squint at—harbour by harbour and street by street. But now he was getting to the end of the box. He had saved the best one for the last.

"Here's quite a good one," he said, handing it to her between forefinger and thumb.

She thought it was good too. An old grey house down by a waterfront. On one side of the door the pale, peeling torso of a ship's figurehead—all blues, sick whites, the nose missing, the hair like badly-piled snakes. The remains of the face were placid; it was a face that gave distance its due. Also, the paint of the eyes had flaked off. And on the other side of the doorway, there was a tall narrow window, and behind the window, behind the smeared glass, a little girl with pale snaggy hair and a round deprived face. It seemed strange that a face could be so perfectly round and at the same time so perfectly deprived. Just as it seemed strange that she, Clare, should so often be unhappy in quite a different sort of house, in this house, here, where the sun shone on the handsome black-and-white tile floor (superimposing its own squares of light), where she could even look out into a garden while she washed the dishes—a beautiful garden (even as gardens go) and in winter beautiful too, in fact in winter a graphic garden, the black branches, the vertical black boards of the fences, all with their epaulets of snow. She looked at the little girl in her leaning sad beautiful blue-grey and probably smelly harbour house, and felt some guilt that she could find such a picture beautiful. Tourists were said to cope with the same kinds of feelings in places like Naples and in the poorer parts of Rome.

"It really captures the poverty and the fog," she said.

"It does," he said.

"Will you have your tea now then?" she asked him. He shoved over his cup.

The tea sprang from the spout in a high clear arch.

"Like a little boy seeing how far he can make it go," she said.

"It is," he said. He looked at it down in the cup. "It *looks* like something done by a little boy, too," he said. "You never make it strong enough." He shoved it back to her. "For God's sake, Clare, steep it a little."

She steeped it till it looked like consommé.

"Is it OK now?"

"Better than it *was*, anyway."

From one extreme to the other, was what he was thinking though. He wished she wouldn't wear those over-sized sad sad cardigans. She had no right to look so vulnerable, so sloppy. Her face was very young looking, her straight hair was pulled back into an elastic band. But her stomach looked three months pregnant. She hadn't had a baby for years, all their children were now in school, and here she slopped around, forever looking three months pregnant. He found he was looking forward to the next lap of the tour and all the airline stewardesses.

"I hardly think about you when you're gone," she

76

said. "I mean I never worry or wonder about what you're doing in the evenings, or anything."

"I never worry or wonder about what you're doing in the evenings, *either*," he said, "because I know you're never doing anything."

"I have a rich fantasy life," she said.

"I daresay you need it."

"When will you be back then?" she asked him.

"Two weeks."

Now he was gathered together at the door, and stood flanked by matching graduated luggage. His raincoat, on his arm, was folded neat as a flag.

"I love you," he said dutifully.

She couldn't bring herself to say anything one way or the other. So she tenderly patted his face.

He pried his tongue into her mouth when they kissed good-bye. But while he was kissing her she could feel him looking at the clock over her shoulder.

"I love you, I love you, I love you," Clare thought, walking in her high boots along the wet leaf-littered streets. It wasn't her husband she was thinking of, but somebody else's. A man who crawled on his stomach through her blood, kneed his way up and down her system, was on her, in her, night and day, in her mind. A speck of plane flew high overhead, very high up in that sky of stomach-dropping blue. Maybe it was the plane her husband was on, maybe he was at this very moment being lulled by acquamarine music, maybe he was at this very moment being leaned down to, being served airline cookies—little cellophane packs of scalloped circles stuck together with oversweet frosting fill and embossed with maple leaves. He could have them.

While she was making supper her children changed themselves into magicians. They came to the table with long black eyebrows and moustaches that went up into commas, and pointed black beards. They kept making faces at her. "God, you look repulsive," she told them. They were delighted. They couldn't hear it often enough.

"Are we really repulsive?" they kept saying.

"Yes," she kept saying back.

And at bedtime, as she was wiping the black from the face of one of them, from the face of Martin, the oldest one, she was thinking of the husband of her friend. Her desire for him was quite unbearable sometimes. She was thinking of how she loved him, when suddenly, without warning, she said out loud, "I love you." Her son, thinking it was meant for him, smiled at her sweetly. Swept by guilt, she held him to her for a moment, terribly tightly.

Her friend's husband was named Don. An ordinary name. An ordinary person. No! Not an ordinary person! Not even ordinary-*looking* once you got to know him. And *he* had such a way of looking at people. Or at least he had such a way of looking at her. A look that took you in entirely, enclosed you. She remembered being a small child and standing barefoot on a sheet of brown paper while her father held a pencil up close against each foot, and described each foot with the pencil, so that he could take the pictures of her feet out in his pocket and come back bringing new shoes. She had been delighted with those pictures of her feet. The way Don looked at her, she felt he saw her exactly as she was, his look described her, and yet she felt such deep approval in his eyes. He treated her with the gentle courtesy one might show to a beloved child. She remembered she had gone to their house to deliver something, some books, late one raining Sunday afternoon. And she had stood out on their white porch with the sky all dark behind her, and her maroon leather shoes had been rained on till they had turned the colour of wine, and she had been shaking the rain out of her coat when he had opened the door to her, but she hadn't been able to shake the happiness out of her eyes. She had always felt that he was ten times more interesting and ten times less pretentious than anyone else. And apart from that, and apart from all the sexual feeling, she had always felt that he was *good*. He had held the door open for her and she had preceded him into the summer dimness of his house. And there had been such a curious smell in the interior of that house, a smell of old socks and fallen flowers. His wife was away. She had known that, known that, known that, when she had cunningly come, returning his books. She didn't see any of the old socks, but she saw little collars of fallen petals around all the vases in the living room. In the kitchen there was a little more light. Not much, but a little. Big windows looked out into a garden of soppy tropical greens and the rain dribbled down them while he put on water for tea.

"Which tea will it be?" he had asked her. "Formosa Oolong? Lapsang Souchong? Jasmine? St. John's Wort?"

They had decided on a blend of Jasmine and St. John's Wort.

"St. John's Wort is like a field of hay," he had said. "You're not allergic to hay, are you?"

No, she had assured him, she wasn't allergic to anything. And she had hoped this would raise her stock with him. The Jasmine flowers had floated like bits of discoloured paper among the grasses in her cup of tea.

And some time later, walking home in the rain, past all the sopping wet gardens, she had felt that she should think some sobering thoughts and douse the happiness in her face before she got back to her husband and children.

On the porch she had taken off her shoes, squeaky

with wet, and had come into the house bare-foot. A wet-footed, white-footed, bare-footed truant. But her children had been watching television and her husband had been reading the paper. They had hardly looked at her at all, and she had gone into the kitchen to start supper, pirouetting as she had cooked and cleaned up, leaping across the chess-board linoleum floor with a violent silent joy. And the happiness inside her! But now she was safer with it. She could push it out of her face and back onto a secret simmer and make it last for hours and no-one would know it was there. She felt happy the way a child can feel happy—without a reason, without knowing a reason and with no need to know a reason.

And so she had sometimes seen him since. Him and his wife, Frances, who was her friend. Frances appreciated him, anyone could see that. And besides, Frances was a warm and attractive person herself. And so Clare went on, would go on forever, feeling that way about him, feeling that deep submerged bond between them, but nothing would ever come of it.

Now all the magicians were asleep. Their moustaches and beards had been creamed away, their faces were upturned, fair, flushed, flung this way and that. She was getting ready for bed herself, had brushed her hair, had figure-eighted an elastic band around it, and was now standing in front of the bathroom mirror, clowning her face with cream. The nightly circus of the no-longer-young. Next week she was invited to a party where Don and Frances would also be. She would wear her African print dress, and her hair hanging straight, and she would be feeling too happy to need jewelry. She was *that* young, anyway, that she could still get by on clean hair and happiness. Downstairs, the phone rang, making her jump. She ran down into the coldness of the hall. She jerked one of her husband's old raincoats off a hanger and was still working herself into it as she picked up the receiver and said hello.

"May I speak to Clare Stanzel?" A man's voice asked her.

"Clare Stanzel speaking."

"Clare! Is it really you?"

"Yes," she said, "but who's this?"

"Someone who loves you very much."

That narrows the field, she thought, but it was not a voice she recognized.

She said: "There can't be that many people who love me very much."

He said: "There can't be that many people who love you as much as *I* do."

A pause followed this gallant remark.

"Keep saying nice things," she instructed him finally, "maybe after a while I'll figure out who you are."

He laughed and then she knew him.

"Wilf Dasgupta!"

"Wilf Dasgupta it is," he said, sounding even more delighted than she did.

"Good to hear from you, Wilf."

"It's been too long," he said. "How's Rawge?"

"Rawge is well. Travelling at the moment."

"And the children?"

"Sleeping. But they're fine too. They were magicians at supper tonight."

"Magicians," he said. "And you?"

"Pardon?"

"And how are you?"

"All right," she said. "Fine. Very well, as a matter of fact."

A skeptical silence ensued. She remembered how he used silences to browbeat you into confessing how you *really* felt. She felt a need to quickly pour words into the void.

"It's strange, I was thinking of you just the other night," she said. She knew he would like that. And besides, it was true.

"What were you thinking?"

"Well, you remember that beautiful art book you gave us when we were married?" she asked him. "We still have it," she continued—she was making it sound as if they made a practice of throwing their beautiful art books out with the garbage or something —"and I was just passing by the bookshelf—"; by now she was wishing she had never started on this, for her thought of Wilf as she had passed by the bookshelf had been a feeling of irritation at the tyranny of his love, at his insistence on beauty, and she had even taken the book down and had read the impassioned dedication he had written to her and Roger on their marriage, telling them how beautiful they were, how miraculous it was that these two beautiful people should have found each other and should now be joined together, and she had closed the book with a real slap of anger. "And?" Wilf was saying, pleased as punch, by now certain he sniffed the scent of a beautiful dénouement. "Well, I noticed how it—how the book—was sticking a little out from the shelf—" She paused, by now regretting her whole contribution to this conversation. She wanted quickly to finish it. She finished: "—and so I shoved it back in."

"That's what you do to me," Wilf said in a heavy swinging voice, "shove me back on the shelf."

She couldn't answer this. She could only think of Wilf in his Montreal studio. Of his tender drawings of nude pregnant negresses up high on the walls. Of the dark nipples, sturdy as gumdrops, hung in the gleaming brown slings of the breasts. Of Wilf, standing barefoot, serving, at just the right moment of the day, when the sun lay across the low black table in the strong-smelling studio, the little glasses of apricot brandy that went down the throat with an oversweet slippery sting. Of the holes at the shoulder of his shirt where his pet bird sometimes sat and clawed. Of the free-form bird-cage he had made for the bird, but which the bird had never taken to. Of an older black wire bird-cage (which the bird had never taken to either), that Wilf had later converted into a portable liquor cabinet, housing half a dozen tall-necked bottles, and of how he used to swing the cage back and forth in front of them, saying, "What'll you have? Port? Sherry? Madeira?" And then he would sing in a cracked satanic Bengalee falsetto, "Have some Madeira, my dear . . . ," and she remembered too his great bowls of fruit that he washed at the old sink where he apparently also washed himself and mixed his paints, and of how good the fruits always looked when he brought them round, clear-beaded with water. And later, coming down into the suppertime dark and the snow-thickened streets, they had felt their eyes were over-tired, over-bright, that everything about Wilf and his studio always came on too strong—the dogmatic batiks, the tangled plants, the raucous tyrannical bird. Even the tenderness of the nude pregnant negresses, up there on the walls in small worlds of their own, even that came on too strong. And Wilf had played ragas long before anyone else, long before they had become fashionable in the West, for his father had come from Bombay, and the fact that his mother was a hard-shell Canadian Baptist hadn't cancelled this out. In fact, in Wilf, nothing had been cancelled out.

"Clare," Wilf was saying, with a kind of deliberate urgency on the other end of the telephone line.

She hugged the raincoat very tightly around her and waited.

"Clare, you know I care for you and Rawge very much."

"Yes, Wilf."

"But about *you*, Clare, *for you*, Clare, I've always felt

83

something very special, ever since I first met you, ever since you opened the door to me that time when you were staying at the Weinbergs'.... "How old were you then, Clare? Twenty? You were very beautiful then, you know that, and you also know, and *I* know that *you* know, that I don't mean beauty in any outside ordinary surface sense, I mean *real* beauty." He paused a moment. His voice had begun to sound charged. He said finally: "I felt that you were good."

"But I'm a mixture of good and bad!" she cried. "Like everyone else!"

"I know what I know," he said, in his inscrutable stubborn voice. There was both Bombay and Baptist in that voice.

"I think you tried to put some kind of halo around me," she said.

"No, no! I didn't try to sanctify you, I didn't try to deify you, I just know what I saw! I feel that there's a place in *my heart* for you, just as there is a place in *your heart* for me, that no-one else will ever occupy, in either of us; that there is an area, a territory, a *country*, if you like, where only you and I meet. A spiritual bond, if you like."

She didn't know if she liked or not. Still she felt a need to say, "Wilf, would you care to come over and have some tea or something?"

"Clare, I'm here for the opening of an exhibition of a friend of mine. You remember my good and beautiful friend, Jean-Luc? Yes? Well, he's having a one-man show here at the Wells Gallery, and now here I am at a party in his honour, here at the Cattleys' until I take the train back very late tonight."

There was a pause.

"But to hell with the party!" he cried suddenly. "*You* are more important than a party! I'll come and see you!"

Clare didn't see how a cup of tea could compete with a party. Even a cup of tea with her. Aloud she said: "I don't want to take you away from your party, Wilf." This was the truth.

"But of course I'll come!" he insisted. "One moment. Someone here drives me over. Can you hold the line?"

She could hold the line. She could also suddenly hear a great avalanche of talk in the background, as if double doors had just been opened. Then, after a time, the talk stopped; the double doors must have closed. She heard him pick up the phone again.

"Clare," he said. Now his voice sounded low, confidential. He sounded like some sort of salesman. "There seem to be some complications here, my little one, so I don't think I'll be able to see you this time, but I'm going to be writing to you."

"Fine, Wilf. I look forward to seeing you another time. It's pretty late right now anyway." Again true.

"Why haven't you ever written to me?" he demanded suddenly. His voice was strong with claims.

"But Wilf, I never write to *anyone*."

"But that's putting me with everyone else!"

Dammit, he *was* with everyone else. This time she refused to answer.

"Clare," he said, after a silence, "Will you do something for me?"

"I'll try," she said warily. She wanted to know what it was first though.

"Remember that I love you," he said.

"Yes, Wilf, thank you, I'll remember."

"I love you."

"Yes, Wilf, thank you. And thank you for calling." By now she was feeling very old.

"Good-bye then, Clare."

"Good-bye, Wilf," she said, and she quickly put down the phone. And then she fled, actually fled, up the stairs, pulling the old raincoat off her as she ran, and pelting it into a pile of dirty laundry at the top of the stairs. Then she bounced onto her bed, and pulled the covers up quickly before she had time to get cold.

She snapped out the light, and lay at attention under the blankets.

But inside her, her heart was beating like a mad bird in the cage of her ribs. And for a long time she couldn't get to sleep. She knew Wilf's need to think he loved people. She knew how he needed to think that things were beautiful and good. She knew it didn't have anything to do with her, any more than the fact that his paintings shone out at you had anything to do with the canvas they were painted on. But this is what bothered her, lying there in the bed: if it didn't have anything to do with her, and if it didn't mean anything, then why did she feel so angry? And why did she feel as if something had been taken away from her? Why were her eyes stinging in her cold-creamed face? Why did she feel as if she had been robbed?

THE NEEDLE'S EYE

The Salon Pauline dealt with hair in two ways. You could have it done up—in the hairdressing section, or you could have it pulled out—in the Electrolysis Room. In the hairdressing section, facing long walls of mirrors, rows of women in pink choir-boy smocks sat watching their hair being ministered to, sat watching their hair being frosted, tipped, streaked, combed, teased. While they watched they were lulled by pastel colours, Musak, trolleys of nail-polish. Women who came to have their hair pulled *out*, on the other hand, were treated almost like medical patients. It was the difference between a purge and a celebration. At the curved pink-and-white candy-striped Beauty Bar, they were met by a technician in a white coat who led them through the hairdressing section and down into the bright white heart of the emporium; the Electrolysis Room was sunk like a clinic in the bottom of a bordello, and the women who were bound for it smiled shy, ironic smiles. They were generally at the age when the body begins, physiologically, to get its wires crossed, when the hair on the head is beginning to thin out, while other, unwanted hair has begun to sprout in new territories, they were generally at the age when the body begins to betray itself. They carried the knowledge of this betrayal with them, briskly, shyly, toward the selective sting of the needle, toward the wonders of technology.

Toward the end of August, Margaret Kalbfleisch waited in the Electrolysis Room, waited for her clients who, one by one, greeted her with pretty much the same words: "Well! And how was the vacation?"

"Vacation?" she cried, smoothing down the white sheet on the little surgical table, smoothing down the front of the white lab coat that she always wore, "I had a *visitor*." She made the word "visitor" sound grim.

After that, the conversation invariably went like this:

"Oh. A relative?"

"It was no relative," said Margaret Kalbfleisch.

"A friend, then?"

"It was no friend."

"*Who*, then?"

"It was a client."

"A *client*!"

"Stranded at the airport," Margaret Kalbfleisch said.

"But how? Surely, if she's a client, she lives *here*?"

"Just returned from Europe. Only five dollars in her pocket. And her apartment still sub-let to someone else."

"But that seems like a terrible imposition! Surely she had friends she could have stayed with?"

"She said all her friends were away."

"In Europe too, I suppose. . . ."

"Probably," Margaret Kalbfleisch said, getting the machine ready.

"Did you know her a little? Personally, I mean?"

"Oh, we'd had coffee together a few times. But I'd never been to her apartment or anything."

"But whatever gave her the idea she had the right to move in on *you* like that? And how could you let her do it?"

"Well, she said it was just for the one night, see. She said she would go to the bank first thing next morning and then she would take out some money and move into a hotel."

"And she didn't?"

"*She spent the whole next day sunning herself in my back yard!*"

"And the day after that?"

"She went back to work. And when she came to my house for supper that night she said she'd been so rushed all day that she hadn't had time to go to the bank."

"Incredible!"

"And the day after that it seemed to have slipped her mind. On top of that, she brought me a guest for dinner."

"I can hardly believe it. *Who*, in heaven's name?"

"Her daughter. Not a bad kid. Considering the mother. Lives in a student residence somewhere. The night after *that*, she started in on me about going on a camping trip with her. She said it would do *my children* good. 'Poor little darlings,' she said. 'They never get any country air.' 'Listen,' I said to her. 'They've been for lots of picnics in the country. The last thing they need right now, with Robbie's asthma, is an overnight camping trip among the goldenrod.' 'Oh come on, Margaret,' she said. 'You know they'd love it. You've got to think of *them*.' 'I *am* thinking of them,' I said. 'And I happen to know what's best.' But do you think she'd take that for an answer? Not her! The next day she phoned me *three times* from her office trying to persuade me to go with her. And that night she brought her daughter to supper again and it was her daughter who finally let the cat out of the bag. *She* was still going on at me about going, and I was still saying No, and then her daughter said, 'Mum, if you go alone, how will you ever get the tent up?' And then *she* said, casual as could be, 'Oh, I'll find someone to help me.' So that was why she wanted me to go, you see! She wanted me to put her tent up for her!"

"This is really fantastic."

"Well, she went off Friday evening. Said she'd be back Sunday night. I was so glad she was gone. Even the kids were glad. Do you know that for the whole time she stayed at my house, she didn't once make her own bed or offer to wash the dishes?"

"I don't see why you put up with her."

"Well, she was a client, you see. I thought she might make some trouble for me at work. I don't want to lose my job."

"Yes, but you haven't done anything wrong?"

"No, but she might make up some story about me. You never know."

"What could she *say*, though?"

"Oh, God knows. But if it was her word against my word, who'd ever listen to me? I got my sister to look up her salary at the civil service. And do you know what she makes? She makes five times the salary I do! I make four thousand a year. She makes twenty thousand."

"Good Lord, I hope she left you some money then."

"Ten dollars. And a bottle of cologne for my little girl. And a pair of airline sockettes with BOAC on them for Robbie. Also a package of hot-dog rolls and a bunch of brown bananas left over from her week-end trip."

"She *did* come back on Sunday night, then."

"Yup."

"What happened then?"

"I was lying on the sofa. 'What's the matter with you?' she said. 'I'm tired,' I said. So she went out to the refrigerator and got herself a piece of chocolate cake and a bottle of coke. 'How'd you make out setting up the tent?' I said. 'Oh, I slept in the car,' she said. I didn't say a word. Finally she said: 'I feel I'm imposing on you.' I didn't say a word to that either. 'So I'll be leaving in the morning,' she said. 'That'll be fine, then,' I said. It was the last night of my vacation anyway. Maybe she was afraid that if she stayed any longer she might be stuck with baby-sitting my kids."

"More than likely. And did she leave the next morning?"

"All up and packed and ready to go before I was ready to leave for work."

"Has she been in for an appointment since?"

"She doesn't have an appointment until next week. And I've no idea where she's staying. Her apartment's still sub-let for at least another two weeks, as far as I know."

"Well, I wouldn't worry about her if I were you."

"I don't intend to."

Margaret Kalbfleisch knew things about her clients; her clients knew things about her. They knew her as a stocky blonde woman with deep-set tired eyes. They knew that she was a widow, that her husband had died young of something drawn-out and painful—cancer or kidney disease or something like that, that she had been left alone with two small children and an ancient father to support. They also knew that her husband's death had set off a chain of deaths (on both sides of the family); two weeks after Margaret Kalbfleisch's husband had died, the husband's father became ill with pneumonia and didn't last a week. Three days after *his* death, driving to another town to pick up some relatives for the funeral, Margaret Kalbfleisch's sister had been killed in a three-car collision. Unable to bear such an orgy of grief, Margaret Kalbfleisch's mother had had a stroke. She, though, had lasted longer, and had not died until the following year. Most of the clients also knew that Margaret Kalbfleisch had been born and raised in a small town in the midwest. Some of them even knew that her father had fought in the First World War, that he had been a year in a German prison camp, that he had come home, moody and strange, to father seven children, and that even now, as a very old man, he sometimes sat and peeled potatoes at the kitchen table and gouged out the potato-eyes, pretending they were the eyes of Germans. He had been against her marriage to a Jew, though, (*his* war with the Germans had had nothing to do with the Jews, he had told her). Her father had never allowed his children to talk back. Once when Margaret, aged ten or eleven, had been treated unjustly by one of the adults in their town, she had been forced to go back to the woman and apologize. 'For what?' she had cried. 'She's the one who should apologize to me!' 'Do what I say!' her father had commanded her. There were times when, in a fury, she had gone out to the kitchen garden and fiercely pulled weeds in order to calm herself. Years later, when her husband was in hospital, dying, she had read in the newspaper about a course for electrolysis technicians. It had seemed just the thing—both for widowhood and rage. She applied, and finished the course in record time. In fact she was already installed in a beauty parlour several weeks before he died. She had had a pale green wool dress that he had liked in those days, and although it was winter, she seemed like someone who didn't need to follow rules, she was like a god, competent and coat-less, moving from heated car to heated hospital to heated funeral parlour to heated church, wearing only a rose-coloured cardigan over the green wool dress, and small black high-heeled boots with bracelets of brown fur around the ankles, and sometimes, in a kind of token homage to the elements, a white satin headscarf that had enshrined in its pattern something that reminded her of her childhood—something glowing and Catholic and inflamed. When human life had been running down all around her, her memory was that the machines had never worked better—her husband's kidney-machine, the car, her watch, the oven-timer, the cuckoo-clock, the machine that plucked the hairs from the faces of the women—everything ticked and ran.

The clients, lying on the little surgical table, often had tears in their eyes. Not because of her story, but because of the needle. Although her story was sad enough. Most of them were thinking, nine times out of ten, "There, but for the grace of God, go I" and she, in a kind of un-knowing, half-knowing counterpoint, was thinking, "Ours not to reason why," as the needle moved in on hairs around the circumference of nipples, as the needle moved in on hairs at the tops of thighs. There was one client, a Mrs. Duval, a fat, white-skinned, black-haired woman who had a fairly heavy growth on the sides of her face. But it was the hairs on her nipples that she wanted to have pulled out. She lay back patiently, one graceful white hand placed between her great spilled wall-eyed breasts, the hand doing double duty, holding her crucifix in place and at the same time covering a large red raised patch of eczema that Margaret Kalbfleisch had once glimpsed in the cleavage. She had tried to convince Mrs. Duval that the real problem was on the face, but Mrs. Duval, her great beautiful dark eyes shining with stubborness, did not want the needle on any place other than her breasts. And then there was Coretta Fullerton, the client she had so unwisely be-friended. Coretta Fullerton wanted the needle nearly everywhere. She was one of those small blonde women with slightly rough skin who seem to get very hairy quite young. For years, she told Margaret Kalbfleisch, she had simply got by on her blondeness, but one day when she could afford it, she had decided to come in and get "the works" . . . the thighs done, the eyebrows thinned out, the upper lip done, under the chin, and what she called her "side-burns." It had been a long job, which partly accounted for the fact that they had got to be friends. "Of course you don't meet many men in this business," Coretta Fullerton had once remarked, with fellow-feeling, and Margaret Kalbfleisch had replied in her dead-pan voice, "No, that's true. Only the male hairdressers." And they had both laughed.

The strange thing was, Margaret Kalbfleisch had been quite happy the night Coretta's call had come from the airport. Her own vacation had been restful but uneventful, and the thought that someone as dazzling and lively as Coretta Fullerton was coming to spend the night had excited and pleased her. "We're having a visitor," she had said to her father as she put down the phone, "I'll sleep on the chesterfield in the living-room and she can have my bed." He had looked distressed. Anything unusual upset him. "It'll only be for one night," she had told him, "and she's a very interesting person." And then Coretta Fullerton had arrived, looking tanned and brisk, wearing a white blouse embroidered with white vines and flowers, red velvet pants with a dark red rose of sweat budding between the thighs, and high-heeled Spanish sandals that looked as if they had been made from sliced-up parts of hand-tooled Spanish purses. She had had several trunks and suitcases along too, as well as two flight-bags stuffed with souvenirs. These she had unpacked and displayed for Margaret Kalbfleisch. She had also unpacked a bottle of Portuguese vinho rosé that she had toasted her return to the country with. It was the first and last taste of the grape during her visit. The rest of the time, instead of toasting her return, she had toasted herself, lying in Margaret Kalbfleisch's back yard, and turning her Spanish-brown body this way and that way to Margaret Kalbfleisch's share of the sun. And after that first day, after she had returned to work, the first thing Coretta would do when she got back from the office in the late afternoon was take a shower and get into her bikini and take a coke from the fridge and go out and sit in the lawn-chair in the back yard. Margaret Kalbfleisch, busy in the kitchen making the supper, got to hate the sight of that little blue and white kerchief-bikini, got to hate the sight of it on that brown body in that white chair on that green grass, and sometimes as she looked out the window at her 'guest', the bottle of coke in the tanned, ringed hand reminded her of the bottle of dark urine under her sick husband's bed during those last bad days when all the clear hospital fluids that had so ceaselessly dripped into his body had been converted into dark and frightening waste.

After Coretta Fullerton left her house, Margaret Kalbfleisch did not hear from her again. And when the day of Coretta's appointment finally arrived, she managed well enough with her. (Coretta was as talkative as ever. And she seemed to feel no guilt). It was with Mrs. Duval, whose appointment had followed Coretta's, it was with kind, gentle Mrs. Duval, with the hand hiding the eczema and holding the cross, that Margaret Kalbfleisch had suddenly felt afraid. At first she was simply afraid that she would reach down and tear the hand away from the eczema and the cross. But soon she became afraid she would do Mrs. Duval some damage with the needle, that she would bring the needle up from the nipple, all the way up to the face, that the needle would go for the fine hair-like lines in the iris of Mrs. Duval's large and beautiful eye. After Mrs. Duval had gone, Margaret Kalbfleisch found that her hands were wet with sweat.

The next time Coretta Fullerton came in for an appointment, Margaret Kalbfleisch again managed well with her—it was only with the woman who directly preceded her, a slim dark woman named Mrs. Lederer,

95

and the woman who directly followed her, a kindly soul who was called Miss Grant, that Margaret Kalbfleisch had felt nervous. Gradually though, the anxiety spread, eddying out to include nearly all the women and leaving Coretta at the centre, a dropped stone, unaware and unafraid and in no danger. Although some days were better than others, Margaret Kalbfleisch became quite desperate. She began to dream of giving up her job. But she could not. It was strange to think that she had once got such satisfaction and release from it, it was strange to think that the needle, once the perfect instrument for both widowhood and rage, had betrayed her. Sometimes she felt shadowed by some great all-seeing spirit that was more powerful than all the poverties of her childhood but which was somehow connected to them. Sometimes she felt that this spirit was the spirit of justice, but sometimes she felt bitter, sometimes she felt it was the spirit of injustice. And she became convinced that it was one of the tricks of this spirit, this power, this justice, this injustice, that she was forced to continue, to struggle on, to survive, even though the execution of her work had become a trial to her.

"How do you spell 'Easter'?"
    "Capital E . . . then a-s-t-e-r."
    "How do you spell 'mythology'?"
    "M-y-t-h. . . ."
    "Yuh?"
    "O-l. . . ."
    "Yuh?"
    "O-g-y."
    "Do you want to see it when it's finished?"
    "Yes, I'd like to."
After a while he brings it to me. It says:

Dear Bestemor,
Thank you very much for the money you sent me for
Easter. I spent it on a book about mythology. At
school we are studying Africa. I love the shape of
Africa. Today we are going to the science museam
with our father.

Love,
Billie.

"Is it okay?"
    "Good. Yes. She'll like it."

Washing the dishes, I think of Hjordis over there in
that country where the snow looks like maps reaching
for the mountain tops, and then I think of Hjordis
here, last winter, after Karl's father died. She wouldn't

eat much. Mostly she cried and smoked. It's easier when the mother who's crying is not your own. Karl was uncomfortable with her crying; I was not. Whatever fondness my mother-in-law has for me dates from that point in time. I sat with her in the living-room where a suggestion of sunlight was held in the dappled cushions, the dappled wall-prints. Scenes of forests in India and Iran. Wicker furniture. Not the fashionable kind with fat baskety hearts and vines the colour of wheat, but ugly dark brown, old, old wicker, with bandages of black masking tape wound around the ankles of the chairs, two brightly painted wooden tables and a threadbare pale red Persian rug on the floor, and on the wall an early Norwegian *rye* rug with small figures on awkward horses that have legs like yellow stairs, and the pink statistics 1873 and 1875 embedded in the chocolate-coloured wool, and on a low white table two plate-baskets filled with sea-buffed fragments of Noxema glass and beer-bottle glass. These were collected by my mother and I value them, since they could represent Nature's attempt to make Progress beautiful. Let me say here that I have a certain weakness for widows—even for my mother, with whom I have little positive connection. I have a tender recollection, for instance, of the way she lay in the bath-tub on the day of my father's funeral and talked in a dreamy child-like voice, a voice languidly storing up certain emotional provisions ("I won't become one of those widows who drinks," "I won't be taking any pills"). Of course, she was very much a member of her class that day, measuring her courage in decanters and vials, measuring her courage in what she would do without. But then everything is relative— grief, courage, luck, abstinence, plans for the future. And years later, Hjordis and I sat in the living-room together. Outside, the low grey Ottawa sky couldn't seem to let go of its burden of snow, but we, sitting on the Salvation Army sofa, drank tea together, and

Hjordis cried and smoked—and also talked—in that repetitive, self-castigating way in which the bereaved lay claim to their dead. Later she progressed and got bossy, but there was a certain humour then, in her orders, a certain memory of the time when I had been her friend.

Not that we haven't had our crises. And they have a curious pattern, these encounters. Once, in springtime, in May, when Hjordis was staying with us, I went with a friend (Ruth Sarrazin) out to the country, to Liz Crawford's, for a Women's Liberation meeting. It was a sunny Sunday afternoon. Ruth and I had to leave the Crawfords' at 5.30 in order to be back at 6.15 for Hjordis, who wanted to celebrate her country's national day at a Norwegian Embassy cocktail party. All the way back, moving slowly with the traffic coming off the Gatineau Parkway, we were deep in talk—mainly about our therapists, Dr. Sidney Schenkman and Dr. Giovanni Grecco (El Sid and El Grecco). (These conversations were always very satisfying and always the same: Could one ever reconcile sisterhood and therapy? And what about the philosophy of El Sid, the philosophy of El Grecco? Opposed, almost completely opposed!) By the time we pulled up to our house, it was 6.40. Ruth's car took off quickly and I remember running anxiously along the slate-coloured dirt path that separated the cedar hedges. Karl was waiting for me on the back porch, like a captain on the bridge of his ship. I ran up the stairs toward him. "Mor is very angry with you," he said, in a low warning voice. I caught a glimpse of her then, through glass, through the living-room window that looked out on the porch; she was at the far end of the room, centred against the light of the three bay windows, very dressed-up—shackled in purple and stiff with rage. Properly warned, I ran through the kitchen, not daring to call her "Hjordis," reduced by guilt and fear to calling, *Mor darling*! I'm sorry I'm late, but the

99

traffic—!" I ran in under the romanesque archway to the living-room.

We approached each other, then, the one supple with supplication, the other still stiff as an avenging Dresden doll, two spots of colour (rouge? rage?) high on her white cheeks, a burning cigarette held out at an angle from her best dress.

"Don't speak to me!" she hissed, marching past me. "You've ruined the Seventeenth of May for me!"

"But Mor! The traffic—"

"I won't be going," she said to Karl, ignoring me. "The day has been ruined. I'm going up to my room."

"Mor!" Karl cried. "Be reasonable! You've heard Anna say that the traffic was bad. . . ."

"She should have started out earlier then," she said to her interpreter.

"We started out over an hour ago! We thought we had plenty of time!"

"I'm going up to my room."

"There's no point in coming too early to these cocktail parties anyway. . . ."

"Most people won't start arriving until about eight. . . ."

"They go on all evening. . . ."

"Anna has said she's sorry. . . ."

"*I won't be going.*"

I started to shout then. I, who had never shouted at her before, I took her by the shoulders and started to shout:

"LISTEN, I'VE TOLD YOU, WE STARTED OUT IN PLENTY OF TIME, THE TRAFFIC WAS BAD, WE DID OUR BEST!"

The old Nordic eyes narrowed, but Karl's eyes cheered us both on. Behind their earnest mediating blue, I sighted a surprising speck on the horizon: he wanted the wife and the mother to destroy each other.

"I suppose you'll be hitting me next," she said.

"I DON'T CARE ENOUGH ABOUT YOU TO HIT YOU!" I shouted, not caring.

Looking both very wounded and very satisfied, she turned on her heel and started up to her room.

"Don't go after her," I said to Karl.

We paced and waited.

She came down sooner than we had dared to hope—powdered, dabbed, red-eyed, contrite.

"Anna!" she cried, taking me in her arms. We patted each other. We apologized. We took each other's measure.

She went off, then, to celebrate the day Norway got its constitution.

The other incident was earlier. At her house on the prairie. (A house well oiled by floor wax and polish and cleanser. A house containing corner-cupboards filled with Norwegian knick-knacks; also a painting, done during one of the winters of the war, of a park in Oslo. There are what look like white bandages wound around the trunks of the trees in the park, for the blackout—really, Karl has told me, these "bandages" are wide rings of white paint—and because of the background of snow, and because of the painter's gifts—or limitations—these trees seem to be cut in parts and floating in air, giving a gently surrealist quality to a traditional scene and technique. In a world of brass candlesticks and hand-carved trolls, this painting stands out in my mind as something very fine.) Hjordis had got tired of a framed clipping from the Oslo evening newspaper, *Aftenposten*, the historic May 1945 edition, announcing the end of the war. "You can take that old thing down," she said. "I'm tired of it. If you'd like to put some photos of the children in the frame, go right ahead. . . ." Then she went off with Karl to visit some friends. I took out the box of photos—the early grainy ones of me in my nightgown holding secret-faced Shaun in my arms;

several of older fatter babies examining their toes in wells of light; Shaun standing in diapers with a proprietary hand on the toilet (the King of the Toilet); Shaun and Billie bundled up in sleds and wearing woollen helmets and pulled by grandparents; Karl flanked by two naked white-haired children at the edge of a grey lake. All afternoon I cut, pasted, made my collage. . . . When Karl and Hjordis came back at 4.30 I was just fitting it all into the frame.

Very nice, they both said. And then Karl said, "Oh, by the way, what did you do with the clipping from the *Aftenposten*?"

"Well, it's just here. . . ."

"*Here?* Where?"

"Well . . . *here* . . . under these. . . ."

"You mean you pasted the photographs *on top of* the *Aftenposten*?"

"Well, yes, I . . . I needed a good strong backing . . . and this cardboard that the clipping was on was. . . ."

I covered the past with the future, I'm still not ashamed of that. Karl made a moderately long speech in which the words "expediency" and "sacrilege" appeared once or twice, but Hjordis, unable to decide which she was most—grandmother or patriot—abstained, and went out to the liquor cabinet in the kitchen to get herself a drink.

And here we all are, after she's progressed and got bossy. It's a school morning and Hjordis comes shivering into the kitchen. The kitchen is cold as a barn. The eight o'clock news says that it's twenty below this morning with a wind-chill factor of 48. Hjordis shivers again, in tribute to the cold facts. Her black hair has been pulled back into a shiny black bauble at her neck, but in spite of the blackness of the hair, the eyes are pale and Nordic. Over her royal blue wool dress that has woollen crewel designs on its stand-up collar (Norwegian rajah) she is wearing one of the dark blue and white *luskofter* ("lice sweaters") that she has made herself. Once, I think, she may have had freckles on her face—now they've slid down to her hands. Liver-spots. She strikes me, as always, as part-brigadier, part-little-girl. The eyes are little-girl, the voice is brigadier.

"Coffee," she says loudly, "I need my coffee."

She shivers. Her shiver is an elaborate *frisson*, the shiver of the twenties' flapper, the shiver of her youth. (Strange to think: even in Bergen, with the sea-light slapping itself against the walls, there were Roaring Twenties). Hjordis opens the cookie jar, filled with cookies that she has made since her arrival. It's one of the tragedies of her life that she, who is an exceptional cook, had a husband who was, for the last twenty years of his life, a diabetic. I am one of those uncompromising types who consider this not so much irony as justice. Hjordis knows this. She is cunningly aware of the passionate and pompous attitude of the young. It may be that she is thinking of this now as she shakes a cigarette out of its pack and lights it. "You young people," she says (with despair? with contempt?). "You have no vices." For her it's fairly simple. She has faith. The existential void is filter-tipped. She exhales.

In spite of the fact that she has lived over half her life outside Norway—in Saskatchewan, in Finland, in Pennsylvania, even, for a short time, in Iceland, her voice still carries the cadences of what Karl calls "the Vestcoast" in it, still has a Bergensk lilt.

"Billie's face is dirty," she says now, in her morning megaphone, spooning out her Nescafé.

"I'll wash it before he goes to school."

"You can't wash his face and then send him out into *this* cold weather."

I wash his face.

They go off then, they kiss their grandmother goodbye, they kiss me. Swaddled against the cold with

Norwegian-style hats and scarves from Christmases and birthdays, vintage 1967, 1968, 1969, all knitted by Hjordis, they trot down the hall and kiss Karl.

I open the door. The air is so cold and dry that it pulls at the nostrils. The snowbanks dazzle like salt.

"*Uf*, hurry and close that door before we all freeze to death!" shouts Hjordis.

The children run down the back stairs, bright bright into the white, only hampered a little by their wool-thickened winter bodies.

I close the door.

The east-coast winters, when I was a child, seemed even greater and colder than this one. The snow was laminated by wind. The fishermen knelt on the ice, lowering shredded medallions of flesh to the fish. Their fingers froze. One winter our father was made a Canadian citizen. It was the first year that there were *real* Canadian citizens—before that they were hybrids, they were British subjects as well. Our father was invited to the special ceremonies because he had written a book on the Micmac and Maliseet Indians and had therefore made a contribution to the culture. He went up to Ottawa on the train. A long trip, taking all night. Before he left, we taught him to sing:

O Canada
Glorious and free
O Canada
We stand on guard for thee!

Its mix of warlike stance and Quaker pronouns made him smile; he learned all the verses, which was difficult, one being much like another. The night of the ceremony, we sat around the old Marconi cathedral radio and waited for our father's name to be called. A funny name. Christian Bang. But Bang was one of the rarer Danish names, and therefore better, we thought, than Hansen or Jensen. And when they sang the anthem, we heard his voice ring out above all the others:

> True patriot love
> In all thy sons command!

We were proud of ourselves for having taught him so well.

Later that spring—the leaves had come out on the trees but then it had snowed . . . curious they were, the poplars. The silver underbellies of the leaves blown back. And the snow falling down in front of them. A mix of seasons and light—we were at a party for a painter friend. This painter friend, a man called Cooper Blake, had just returned from a trip to France, where he had been given an honorary doctorate from one of the universities in the south. "Good Evening, Dr. Blake," my father had said, trying out Cooper Blake's new title. And Cooper Blake had smiled and bowed and had replied in his sonorous dead pan voice, to which he had given a touch of French accent for the occasion, "Good Evening, Citizen Bang." My father, delighted, had sat down beside me on the brown sofa in the uneven candlelight, while we held plates of spaghetti and bear-steak on our laps (me, how old? Ten? Braids, knee-socks, spaces between my teeth), and had told me about the French Revolution and *A Tale of Two Cities* and Madame Defarge and her knitting, and how people in those days were called, with touching revolutionary simplicity, "Citizen," and how clever it was, on *many* levels, of Cooper Blake, who had just come back from *France* where he had got a doctor's degree that had *no meaning*, and having heard of the citizenship ceremonies here in Canada, to address *him, Christian Bang,* as "Citizen," which, in this day and age, in this country, *also had no meaning.* . . .

My beloved father, Connoisseur of Ironies. Of course if he were alive today he would see that the quality he most loved in his adopted country has hardened (or flowered) into a kind of nationalism he wouldn't care for. He left Denmark because he couldn't bear its smallness, its neatness, its careful laws. I have a photograph of him, taken the year he was conscripted, in 1920 when he was twenty, marching with his regiment, carrying his gun in that lax distinctive way the Danish Royal Guards carry their guns—cradled prone in their folded arms, as if they were sleeping babies. When he arrived here, the first part of the country he wanted to see was the prairie. The space. The lack of definition. But the people were very definite there. Definite and clear. He retreated to the far edge of the east coast, which looked less amorphous but was really more so. Beneath the solid shapes of hills and trees there was an amorphousness, a despair. It suited him. He settled there.

Karl comes into the kitchen already in his overcoat.

"You forgot to pack my lunch," he says.

"Oh fuck."

Hjordis looks intrigued. "What does this word 'fuck' mean, anyway?" she asks us. "Does it mean what I think it means?"

"Yes," we say in unison. Compatible in word, if not in deed.

"There's no word for it in Norwegian," she says. "No bad word, that is. There's only *samleje* and that's quite a respectable word." She sighs. "Now I could certainly use a bit of this fuck," she says.

Karl and I smile at her, quite tenderly.

Encouraged, her eyes fill up with tears. "You have no idea how hard it is, being a widow. . . ."

"Don't make them all cheese," Karl says to me.

"We're out of salami—"

"I wish you'd keep a list of the things we're running

out of. You know that I'm perfectly willing to pick up things downtown—"

"I *know* that!"

Maybe we don't want to listen to her. Or maybe our bickering is pure compassion, an attempt to show Hjordis that the marriage she longs for may not, after all, have been paradise.

"I hope you two appreciate each other," she sniffles. "Because when death comes, there's no going back. . . ."

Should we be really compassionate and tell her that we haven't had sex for three months? Our eyes meet and decide not to give such a hazardous *coup de grace* to her sexual longings. Karl picks up his briefcase, kisses us both good-bye and leaves.

"Yes," says Hjordis, sighing heavily, after the door closes. "Yes."

Yes, what?

Something in my blood is on guard.

"Make sure you appreciate him," she says. "It isn't good, for example, to give him only cheese in his lunchbox. A man needs variety. Also, he works too hard—"

"People can make choices," I say, trying to strike a jaunty note. Then it occurs to me that she might respond to this by remembering that in the cheeses there were no choices. But no, she hasn't heard me at all, even to misunderstand me.

"Every night, for instance, when he comes home from work, you should see that he has a little nap—"

The mail falls through the slot at the front door. I go out gratefully to get it. There are two letters and a post-card for Hjordis, two notices for Karl.

Hjordis reads her mail.

I open last night's paper, but there's nothing in it to help me, there's nothing in it to make me smile. Once there was. Once I remember reading:

The Queen and Prince Philip sleep in a large double

bed with a silken canopy. They have individual bathrooms and dressing-rooms. They breakfast together (the pats of butter are monogrammed) at 8.15 am in a room overlooking a small flower garden. She pours out his coffee before her own tea.

I pick up Karl's mail. "There are two things that Karl has to go to over the weekend," I say. "A party on Saturday night, a meeting on Sunday afternoon."

"Oh he does too much!" she cries.

She takes up her knitting.

"You young women today, you don't really know how to appreciate a man. When you think of all the things men do for us. We should take good care of our husbands. . . ."

"You were the one who was against Karl and me sleeping in the same bed when we got married," I say, surprising myself.

Hjordis laughs. "It's only a small leap from one bed to the other," she reassures me in her Bergensk lilt. "You didn't listen to me anyway! I'm only an old woman, nobody listens to me."

The knitting needle stabs into the wool, is lassoed. Stab. Lasso. Stab. Lasso.

And the bed looms large in my mind. Somehow Hjordis was able to give Karl the impression that no woman was good enough to sleep with *her son* (how else explain his eternal search for a proper, or improper, candidate? And that is something that I can't even tell her about! . . . mainly from fear that she will say it's my fault). But now, suddenly, it looks almost mathematically clear: Hjordis gave her son the impression that I wasn't good enough for him, and so after we were married, he continued his search for someone who *was*. And as a result of this search, we have moved out of one bed and into two, so in the end his mother got her wish.

"But *why* were you against our sleeping together in

108

the same bed?" She looks surprised I should have to ask. "Because it's not nice for the man when the woman is having her monthly period. Do you think that's nice? Do you think it's nice for him to have to put up with *that?*"

"I don't know whether it's nice or not . . . it's part of life . . . *we* have to put up with it."

She laughs. Something alters. During this whole conversation blood has been thicker than water. Now, suddenly, blood is thicker than blood. But then she remembers that she's crossed the line into the neutral bloodless territory of the woman over 50. She washes her hands of that part of her history. "Thank God that part of my life is over," she says.

I look at her coldly. She's quick, she's noticed. "But do you know something strange, Anna? Before Knut died—whenever he was away at veterinarians' conferences, or out at night with a sick animal—I couldn't sleep, I would be so nervous about being alone—and now that he's . . . gone . . . and I'm alone *all the time*, I'm no longer afraid. Isn't that strange? It's almost as if God is giving me the strength I need. Or perhaps Knut, up there, wherever he is, is blessing me, is making me brave. . . ."

"Maybe you're braver because you're no longer being treated like a little girl, you're responsible for your own life now—"

Her pale eyes meet mine for a moment, quite terrified. "Let's have a drink!" she cries, "Martini Rossi! And put lots of ice in it."

I get out the ice-tray, the wine-glasses. When I hit the lever on the tray (too hard, I must admit), several ice-cubes leap to the floor. Hjordis laughs. My clumsiness magically brings about her recovery. She comes over and embraces me. "Oh, Anna!" she cries, "You are so hopelessly undomestic!" Her embrace is like the embrace of her son. She holds me hard against her; I breathe in the smell of wool and nicotine. She has no smell herself. She must be the cleanest woman in the world.

"Get the ice," she says. "I'll mop up the mess on the floor."

I pick up the ice-cubes and put them into the colander and rinse them. I dump three cubes into each glass. I uncork the Martini Rossi and pour it down on the cubes. I hand Hjordis her glass. She sips from it and gives her girlish shiver.

"Hjordis," I say softly, but not without a certain instructive malice, "didn't you ever want to do anything with your life?"

A curious expression crosses her face. Almost sensual with possibility. She is examining something in her mind and then, being a "realist," throwing it out. She gives her *frisson*, her shiver. She smiles her girlish smile. "Skaal," she says.

Stab.

I stand there, holding my glass close in against me, at my waist. I can feel the coldness of my drink flowering down to its stem. Hjordis shoves the post-card she got in this morning's mail across to me.

Lasso.

"Paradise," she says, smiling. But all I can see is one of those turquoise hotel swimming-pools, floodlit for night use, and in the left-hand corner one of those tropical trees, black against the swimming-pool-coloured sky. . . .

Then I find, over a period of months, a story, then a quotation, then later a map. The story is by Shaun, it's in his grade six work-book. It's called, like a parody-echo of all the primary-school simplicities,

A is for atom, B is for bomb.

A code-phrase for how the times have changed. Then the quotation, under a chapter-heading in Koestler's *The Ghost in the Machine*, from someone called J.

Cravierinha: "I come from a country which does not yet exist." And finally, the map. Made by Billie. Not shaped like his beloved Africa. Not exactly. Shaped more like the head of an antelope, straight on; the names of its countries suggesting influences ranging from Tarzan, through television, and on to the names of certain family friends:

Crowne
Srench
Bloor
Bungo
Mator
Rpray
Neater
Zem
Eno
Brebut
Bibo
Plat
Ruzy
Drub
Zime

A DAY AT THE FRONT, A DAY AT THE BORDER

It is June. 1969. Ten o'clock on a Saturday morning. Right away we are led around to the back where folding chairs have been set up. The first thing I notice is that we are all wearing pants. There are four pairs of shorts (two pairs short shorts, two pairs Bermudas), one pair of long flowered culottes, two pairs of bell-bottom jeans and one pair of pink stretch pants, positioned neatly to one side of the chair as if the wearer were riding up a ski lift, except that the slope behind her is green, not white. All around us are ice-cream-coloured houses angled in various ways on what appears to be continuous lawn. Along a part of this continuous lawn a man is guiding a power mower. The powerful droning is overwhelming. "Saboteur," someone says, and in fact his sabotage is so effective she has to say it twice. Not for him to hear. Just for us. Since no-one wants to go over and tell him to stop, there is nothing left for us to do but to hike our chairs into a smaller circle and start to read the literature.

Down on the grass, sandals and handbags are at odds with each other. The anxious matching of purses to shoes of our mothers' generation is not in evidence here. Handbags are of two types: either handwoven and Greek or hand-tooled and Mexican. If leather, they are of a different leather from their darker or paler leather sandals. Some of the handbags are hanging on the arms of chairs, like horses' nose bags, stuffed with pamphlets, some are lying on the grass, their flaps back, their inner lips curved with great widths of white, the white of papers, the white of revolutionary material from south of the border. The radical student, imported from Toronto especially for this occasion, is passing some of the stuff around. She is saying that the group in Toronto has split the same way the groups in the States have—into Feminists and Marxist Women. She is a Marxist Woman.

Florence Ferrara is saying that two of her boys have just been landed. Somebody says, Good, somebody says, Hooray, somebody else says, Things looked kind of bad there for a while, it looked like Immigration was going to act tough. Florence Ferrara is one of the women who is counselling deserters from the American Army on how to get their landed-immigrant status. She has been involved in marches, demonstrations and sit-ins for years. She could write a guided tour of all the jails from here to Edmonton. Today she is wearing a batik blouse that the colours have bled out of. I imagine Florence Ferrara sitting in jail and the colours bleeding out of her batik blouse, but it is entirely more likely that this has happened at other times—out in the brilliant sun when she was marching or sitting-in or weeding her organic garden. Florence Ferrara is the oldest woman here, she is also the most beautiful and the most dynamic. Some people think she's crazy, some people think she's a show-off, but I am one of her fans. The radical student is about twenty-one and the rest of us must have an average age of thirty-five. All of us who have an average age of thirty-five have small children. Only Florence Ferrara and the radical student are *free*. We discuss this. "It's not the *truth* that shall make ye free," some-one says, "it's *day nurseries*." This brings broad smiles all round. From here the discussion goes predictably on to co-operatives, communes, retreats, abortion. Then Florence Ferrara says that the United States is like the Male—aggressive, power-mad, authoritarian, exploiting—and that Canada, with her long history of welcoming fugitives to the maternal bosom (fugitives running all the way from United Empire Loyalists and slaves to draft resisters and deserters), passive, motherly, dependent, exploited and taken for granted, Canada is the Female.

"And always the last to know," I say.

"How do you mean, Anna?"

"I was thinking of the revolution," I say. "After all, here's all this material from south of the border, these attitudes have been in existence for quite some time there, and not just *there*, but other places too. Finnish women, Dutch women, Swedish women, have all been familiar with this kind of thing for years". Everyone nods. "Do you know what my five-year-old son said to me the other day? He said, Why isn't God a Woman?"

"You should have said, like the suffragettes, *She is!*"

"What *did* you say?"

"I said he was an idea."

"*He!*"

"Correction: I said *God* was an idea."

Liz, sitting beside me, says "*Intellectualizing!*"

So I decide to stop talking for a while. It is true that my kids are inordinately interested in God. They also ask me, with amazing regularity, Does God fart? Because they know I don't *know*. They can ask me questions about sex and know I will tell them everything, I will even dutifully inform them that *sex is fun*, but when they ask me questions about Heaven they know I'm on unsure ground. Not long ago they had a holiday from school. It was raining and they were with me in the kitchen. Billie was sitting at the kitchen table drawing his masterpieces of monsters and explosions. And Shaun was standing at the kitchen door hating God for making it rain.

"That proves God doesn't exist!" he cried out in

anguish. "If he existed he would know that today is a holiday and that I don't want rain!"

"Suppose there is a God," I say, "and I'm not saying that there is or there isn't, because to tell you the truth, I don't know," I say, "but let us say for the purposes of this discussion that there is a God, and let us also say for the purposes of this discussion that one of his jobs as God is to answer people's prayers. Then suppose there is a farmer, right here in the Ottawa valley, who has been praying for rain, but you, Shaun, also right here in the Ottawa valley, have been praying for sun. What's poor old God supposed to do? You see, it's not reasonable to suppose that God could answer everybody's prayers. People aren't praying for the same things! There are many people in the world and they aren't all praying for the same things."

After this, I go on drying dishes, pleased with myself. I believe I have taught my child the most difficult lesson of life, this lesson being that he is not the centre of the universe. And there is a great silence while Billie at the drawing board, Shaun at the door and I at the dishpan contemplate the wisdom of my words.

"I don't care!" Shaun cries out suddenly. "I still hate God because he's ruined my day!"

Can it be that I've wasted my breath?

But Billie, who so far has not said a single word, is about to speak. He continues to draw Batman's cape with five-year-old abandon as he does so. And this is what he says to his older brother:

"It's not *God* you should hate, it's the *farmer*."

I tell this to Dr. Grecco, lying on the cold brown leather of his couch. So he can see how brilliant my children are. You might have tried dealing with their feelings, is all he says.

I have always had great faith in the logic and generosity of children. I even once helped to organize an anti-war action around that faith. It was a children's march held on the day the Canadian Air Force threw its annual air show. The theme of the march was Drop Flowers, Not Bombs, the idea being to embarrass the military with the merciless logic of the child, to wound it with roses in its exposed metal flank. With great enthusiasm I painted piles of posters of airplanes dropping bouquets of roses, zinnias, daisies. But my *pièce de resistance* was a poster of a general with a black walrus moustache (in India ink) and two small square glints in his roving black India-ink eyes. But instead of having military medals and crosses on his chest he was decorated with carnations and daisies hung from v's of striped ribbon. Then in large black letters I painted across the bottom: BOUTONNIERES! PAS CROIX DES GUERRES! This satisfied my passion for protest, decoration and bilingualism all in one fell swoop and later, after the march, I tacked the posters to the wall of the children's playroom where even now I occasionally hear their five-to-eight-year-old friends cry out in astonishment: "Drop flowers, Not bombs. . . . That's crazy!" and "What does this one *here* mean? Is it *French* or something?" My faith in the logic and fair play of children has thus more than once been ruthlessly slapped down. Of course, one can assume that such children have already been corrupted by the system and are not speaking for themselves.

I come to, back to the meeting, and hear Pink Stretch Ski-Pants talking about orgasms. Their sedative effect. Cheaper and more fun than sleeping pills. She will give her husband perfect freedom to have any number of affairs. If only he will also give her the same. I look carefully at Pink Stretch Ski-Pants. Her skin is speckled as a trout's with reddish brown freckles. But it isn't Pink Stretch Ski-Pants who's at this moment a fish. We are the fishes. She's throwing us a line—one of the standard lines, true—nicely festooned with bait. And any moment now, we, an upward avalanche of fishes, are going to rise to the occasion and begin, one by one, to bob for the bait. And any moment now, too, that gentle *esprit de corps* with which we were hatched (like new chicks) from our battered station-waggons will have been distorted into our adhering (like barnacles) to a taut party line. I can see that. I can also see that the analogies are moving from sea to land. Evolution in the Analogy Department. I can make a Saturday's list:

Barnacles
Chicks
Line
Bait
Fish

and this can go on, quite logically, to

Hook

and that to

Pain (which is French for bread. And that is strangely fitting—since everything has its uses).

For instance, if I, a painter, paint from painful experience, then the pain that feeds the painting buys the bread. You can even go on from there and play little bilingual games; as, for example, "Man does not live by *pain* alone."

Now the trend has begun. Several women say that they wouldn't mind if their husbands had affairs. Freedom for all. A tall dark girl called Karen begins a survey. Would you mind? she says to Florence Ferrara. Florence Ferrara says she would not mind. (Ah, but Florence is safe, her husband wouldn't dare, Liz signals with her eyes to me.)

The woman in the flowered culottes says she would not mind.

Maria, the radical student, doubts she'll ever bother to marry, but if she does, No, she would not mind.

Inevitably Karen is going to get to me.

Liz says she doesn't know if she would mind or not. She shrugs. She abstains.

The fine-boned girl says she would not mind.

Karen gets to me.

"Anna?"

"Yes," I say.

"Yes what?" everybody says.

"Yes, I would mind. I mind. I have minded," I tell them, and it occurs to me that I have not only conjugated minding, I have also defined myself as the reactionary of this group.

"How did you find out?" is the first question. I shrug.

"Why did you mind?"

"I don't know why I minded. But I can't lie and say I didn't."

"I cannot tell a lie," says Karen morosely, tapping her pencil against her wine-glass stem. "With my little hatchet—"

"That's it!" Florence Ferrara cries. "Even our political anecdotes come from *down there*! But who knows any stories about Sir John A. Macdonald? Apocryphal or otherwise?"

"We all know that he drank like a fish—" the woman in the flowered culottes says.

Karen raises her wine-glass that was recently a cherry tree and is now once again a wine-glass. "To Sir John A.—" she says.

"Do you feel possessive about your husband?" Maria is asking me.

"Yes."

"Why?"

"I don't know."

"What part of your husband do you feel you own? Arms? Legs? Genitals? What?"

"No part. That's the point. I'm possessive, and he won't be possessed."

Again, "How did you find out?"

"The first time, I got a letter from the woman's husband." And now here I am in the group remembering this letter, remembering how it began, "I am sorry to have to tell you—." Why *tell* me, then? Why ruin my makeshift, make-believe world? I remember that his handwriting was in a script so perfect it looked as if each letter had been shot from a gun to fall precisely on a series of invisible bull's eyes on the pale blue airmail paper.

"What was this woman like?"

Her name was Jocelyn. He had made her write my name and address on the envelope. Her handwriting looked like a poorly done piece of knitting—clots of letters like clots of black wool, then the letters un-ravelling, then being awkwardly knitted up again. Had her husband stood over her, forcing her to humili-ate herself with that plaintive uneasy childish scrawl?

"She was young. She admired him very much. She adored him, as a matter of fact." I speak from the dead centre of experience. But as I do so I am watching their faces all the time, navigating carefully between arousing either pity or contempt. "I was young too," I say "and did not adore him enough." I smile. Very soon they will lift my suffering from me and explain it in sociological terms. Maybe that's what I want. And then I think about how Jocelyn looked. Colour-less lashes, watery pig-like blue eyes, a long Renais-sance face, long shiny caramel hair, centre-parted. Jocelyn, a mixture of pig and madonna.

"Does your husband require a lot of adoration?"

"Quite a lot."

"He sounds like a baby."

"All men are babies," says Karen.

"He exploited that girl," Florence Ferrara says.

"Maybe that girl exploited *him*," I say. Now I am in the beautiful position of having everyone tear him apart while I defend him. Liz gives me a shrewd look. She goes through the literature. "Hold everything, girls!" she cries. The "girls" is a parody of middle-aged women calling each other "girls." "Ah," she says, "here it is, and I quote: 'Since when do revolutionaries exploit each other?'"

"Was that girl a revolutionary?"

"We were all in the anti-war movement together," I say.

"Has he had any, ah, liaisons, since?"

"One," I say.

"That I know of," I add, striking fear into every eye.

"What was the reason this time?"

"He felt he was getting old."

"Jesus! He has no monopoly on that feeling!"

"How'd you find out this time?"

"Through movies and dreams."

"What's that supposed to mean?"

"Do you really want to know?"

"No!" says Liz, saving me.

But it's true. It *was* through movies and dreams. It was that year he was living away from home, working in Quebec. One weekend when we were lying together in bed he told me that he had been to see the movie *Belle de Jour* while he was away. It was a movie I had seen earlier. It was a movie that had upset me. We lay in bed and talked about it in detail. You couldn't tell what was fantasy and what was reality in that movie. Some people said that the key to knowing the difference lay in the sub-titles. Whenever an incident was a fantasy the sub-titles were supposed to have gone into gothic script. What about the audience where the film was made, then, in France, I asked Karl. And where Karl had seen it, in French, without sub-titles, in Quebec? Without sub-titles how did they *know*? Karl and I disagreed on what was fantasy and what was reality.

I said to Karl: "Belle de Jour had a good imagination. Most of the movie just happened in her mind."

Karl said, "I don't agree. I think she really had this crazy gold-toothed lover."

"And you think this lover shot up her husband and crippled him?"

"Sure."

"And blinded him?"

"Yes, Your Honour."

"How do you explain the appearance, then, *in advance of the shooting incident*, of the wheel-chair? Premonition?"

"Coincidence, Your Honour."

"There are no coincidences. Look: the camera lingers over a wheel-chair that Belle de Jour and her husband are passing as they're walking along the street. And later, when the husband has been crippled, he appears to be sitting in the *same* wheel-chair that a long time before, in happier days, they passed in the street. How do you explain that?"

"In all works of art there are mysteries, Your Honour."

I felt disoriented. Up to this point I had imagined *I* was the one on the side of mystery. Now Karl seemed to be changing the terms of reference. I turned anxiously toward him.

"But do you remember what the husband was saying to Belle de Jour around the time they were passing the wheel-chair?"

"No, what?"

"He was saying he thought they should have a child."

"So?"

"Well, my guess is that Belle de Jour was thrown into a panic by the idea of a child, of pregnancy—or maybe simply by the idea of the kind of sexual relationship that could lead to the conceiving of a child—and so she immediately began to have death-wishes against her husband and her eye fell on the wheel-chair and in her own practical, fantastic way she immediately worked up a fantasy around it."

"Putting him in a wheel-chair isn't killing him."

"It's putting him into a place where he can't make her pregnant though. It's putting him into a place where he can't make sexual demands. It's putting him out of commission."

"I'm sure that problem could be handled." I felt him smiling in the dark.

"With a little ingenuity," he said.

"Only with her co-operation, though, Karl."

"Yeah, that's true."

"And the horses were running along with an empty carriage at end of the movie, remember that. To me, that *proves* the whole thing happened in her mind."

"No, I think it really happened. Terrible things can happen in life."

"Did you see it alone?"

"No."

"With a girl?"

"With a girl."

"What's her name?"

"Her name is Giselle and she's teaching me French."

After that, every weekend I said "How's Giselle?" and every weekend he said "Fine." When I asked him if he was attracted to her he said no, he wasn't, she didn't have any breasts. I have since realized that whenever Karl is attracted to a girl he always tells me she hasn't any breasts. This is supposed to allay my anxiety. And how did I find out in the end? Well, he more or less told me. He half-told me. He made a lot of jokes. "Giselle is pretty good in bed," he would say and then he would say he was only joking, that she really wasn't very attractive. A girl for talking French with, not for sleeping with. But one Sunday morning he was polishing his shoes and he called out to me that during the night he had dreamed he was polishing his shoes. Karl, who never dreams, who *says* he never dreams, had dreamed he was polishing his shoes. I stood at the stove holding a warm egg wobbling on a spoon. Patches of wet, small allotments on the world of the egg were disappearing into steam. He said that in his dream he kept applying more polish at the same time that he was trying to shine the polish off. This dream seemed to say that he had a conflict. The whole next week while he was away again I kept thinking about his dream and the next time he came home I said, "You've been sleeping with her." And he said—and it was suddenly as if we were reading a script for an afternoon soap opera—"That's what I've been trying to tell you for the last three months." We have these strange dialogues in instalments. Weeks pass between sentences.

Somebody is saying that the pamphlets should also be printed in French, and then somebody says it's time to go inside for food. We all go in out of the hot sun. On the table there are black olives like round black stones on a wet beach, and sliced tomatoes and a lot of salads. Someone has put on a record of Judy Collins singing the songs of Leonard Cohen. Someone says: "She sings his songs better than he does." Not true, I think. He sings them the right way, he sings them like a child singing himself to sleep.

"Sit beside me, Liz."

Liz collapses on the sofa beside me. She is either sunburned or drunk. Maybe both. Liz is both dogmatic and whimsical. It is a combination that alarms and charms me since it is what I also am. On the other side of me the pale fine-boned girl is telling me that her husband has the emotional age of a child of eight.

Karen is pouring more wine and asking more questions. Each time she fills a glass she gets an answer. "How did your husbands feel about your coming here for the whole day?" It turns out that some husbands felt pleased and proud (paternalism!), some felt anxious (with good reason!), some were patronizing and covered their fear with jokes.

"Anna?"

"He was fairly amenable and somewhat amused.

He looked a little put upon when I said I wouldn't have time to serve everybody breakfast and so I said, 'This isn't so bad, we've been married ten years and this is the first time you've had to look after the kids for the whole day,' and he said. 'Revenge, Revenge, all women ever think of is Revenge!'"

There are several loud moans. One woman who has recently been beckoning her fingers into the air above her head to indicate "in quotes" now brings her fingers down to her face and beckons them beneath her eyes to indicate "in tears."

Now Karen is coming around with the desserts and more questions.

"In what ways do your husbands feel critical of you?"

Some women can't think of any ways their husbands could possibly be critical of them. Incredible. "They lie," Liz says to me.

The dessert, which looks like dirty chunks of foam, is very good. I can see a dreamy diagnostic look in the eyes of at least two of the women. It looks like they are suppressing an insurrectionary impulse to ask for the recipe.

"Hey, Liz, who's the one in the flowered culottes?"

"Eunice Something-or-Other. What Eunice really wants is revolutionary carte blanche to make every man from here to Mexico. To hell with her. She isn't bright enough for this discussion anyway."

Still, I feel some kind of warmth. Especially toward Liz, Maria the Marxist, Florence the Mad-Sane, and myself. But also toward the fine-boned girl with the eight-year-old husband, Eunice of the Flowered Culottes, Pink Stretch Ski-Pants and Karen, the Dark Lady of the Suveys. I wonder, though, why I'm giving everyone a nick-name. I've over-revealed myself, that's why. It's a defence. Funny names for the people I've told too much to. Now Maria is saying that lower-class boys are sexually very uninhibited because of the communal nature of lower-class life. Very few bedrooms. Maybe everybody in the same bedroom. "The lower-class child is very matter-of-fact," Maria says. "Describing the sexual life of his parents he will simply say: 'Daddy gets on top of Mummy and they fuck.'" "Or Mummy gets on top of Daddy," I say. "Anyway, I thought that that was just a myth—the wantonness of the lower classes."

"Well, there are a lot of myths," Maria says dreamily. "Take the widespread belief in the tremendous freedom and frequency of sex among kids in their teens and early twenties, for instance. After all, we too have our hang-ups."

Several of the women look deeply grateful to hear it.

"We should soon be going," Liz whispers to me.

Oh God, I haven't told anywhere near the whole truth. It's true that Karl exploits me, but it is also true that I ask to be exploited. Only Karl and Dr. Grecco know that. Only Karl and Dr. Grecco know that when, in bed, coming toward what might delicately be called the oceanic moment, what I say to Karl is this: "Fuck me! Screw me!" Even, on rare occasions, "Rape me!" We hadn't been married two weeks before I started saying those words to Karl. At first they had an exciting effect on him. "Thank you for saying the things you said," he would say afterwards, with great circumspection. Not saying himself what the words were. But after a while he found that he didn't really like it after all. He began to compliment me on those times I didn't say anything. "You didn't have to say anything that time," he would say. And I know now that I must try to spare him from the words that are both animus and dregs, both dark core and essence, of what's really been happening between men and women since almost forever. Or is that the way it really is? I think you will argue, Sisters, that to wish for exploitation is to have experienced it, since you can't wish for what you don't know. But it's also true that I cannot tell this story to you, sisters in the struggle, I have only been able to tell it to Dr. Grecco. Who is one of the enemy. Who is one of the arch-enemies. A psychoanalyst. Born a man. Raised an Italian. Trained a Freudian. Three strikes against him right from the start. And yet I trust him more than I trust any of you. More even than my three best women friends, one of whom is sometimes Liz. I trust him (and this really is crazy!) even though I know that the circle in which he liberates me is a circle surrounded by walls. I sometimes worry about his wife though. Some of the analytic sessions have been dominated by my concern for her freedom. He implies that this is none of my business and also, perhaps, not my real concern. But if she makes him possible so that he can come to his office and make me possible, who is to say that my liberation is not at the expense of hers?

Maria is saying that one of the "feely" groups in the United States spent six months talking about masturbation. And in unison we all cry out in astonishment, Six months! which is somewhat easier than crying out in astonishment, Masturbation!

Then we gather together our papers and pamphlets and sunglasses and our beautiful handbags from the lands of coups and revolutions and we all go out to the cars. Maria and I are riding with Liz. Maria climbs into the back. I sit in the front. Liz steers a careful course between children playing ball in suburban streets. Maria lounges in the back seat and sighs. I turn and look at her with wary respect. She yawns, stretches. "Well," she says, "that really went very well . . . . Of course all the women there were good at verbalizing . . . . All vaguely left-wing . . . all intelligent . . . well-edu-cated . . . ."

Oh God, she's lumping us all together.

"Whaddayah mean, well-educated? University?"

"Yeah. University."

"I only went to high school," I say.

"Anna was a drop-out nurse," says Liz.

"Now there's a microcosm of the whole male-female thing for you," I say, "the hospital, and how it's run. The nurses are exploited mothers and waitresses. The doctors are the bosses. Nurses: women. Doctors: men. And what is every nurse's dream? To marry a doctor. And what is every woman's dream? To marry a man."

"Well you know it's a funny thing," Maria says, "but in Russia where most of the doctors are now women, doctors don't have much status any more. And they are getting lower salaries."

Incredible, we all say. Incredible.

"I read the other day that some male radical leader—at Berkeley, I think it was—said, "Let them eat cock." Did you read that?"

"Yeah," says Maria. "Who needs that? Who needs the social Darwinism of these latter-day male Marie Antoinettes? You should read Marlene Dixon on this."

"Ah, Mr. Faithful Begg and Mr. Strangeways Pigg, where are you now that we really need you? Where are your representatives in the present age?"

"Who were *they*?" Liz asks me.

"Two nineteenth-century British parliamentarians who tried to get the vote for women. Bertrand Russell writes about them in *Marriage and Morals*."

Liz says: "My problem is I can't think of any men I really like."

Maria says: "And what did you do then?"

"When?"

"After you were a drop-out nurse."

"Oh a little typing. While I sat around on my fanny waiting for Karl to marry me and take care of me forever and ever."

"You exploited *him* then."

"That's right."

"And what do you do now?"

"I paint."

127

Maria looks as if she will have to know what kinds of paintings I paint before she can decide if this is a good thing. Fair enough. Liz's car turns into the street where I live. I can see Maria wondering: Social realism or stripes? In fact, Maria, neither one nor the other. I paint people. People who live in an enchanted doom, mired in paint and indecision. But now we're here. I say good-bye and get out of the car.

In the garden spring is over. The lilac blooms have shrunk into turrets of rusted flowers. Lower down, holes and trenches have been abandoned for yet another approximation of the real thing: the five-o'clock television cartoons. I am very anxious to see Karl. I run up the back stairs, my fat brown legs propelled by guilt and power. Inside, Karl is en route to the bathroom with a pale wet diaper. I can see he is making an effort to greet me with neither pleasure nor reproach. Did he learn this lack of love from me? Or at his own mother's knee? And in any case, why should I think that somewhere, somehow, some woman has been responsible? The truth is, now that I'm here I wonder why I've hurried. All day long (maybe all life long) people have been like mirages. The closer you get to them the more they are not there. I am no exception. Karl is no exception. In the living-room, Shaun and Billie, watching the cartoons, are no exception. Only Tim, standing in the middle of the room, hobbled by his rubber pants, is perhaps an exception. And that part of him that marks him as an oppressor of me and all my kind is hanging there, pristine and perfect and pure. *Ah Tim! Someday that lower hanging nose of yours will be able—at moments both convenient and inconvenient—to grow as long as Pinocchio's. But not till you've reached the age of puberty and lies.* (And that in itself is a lie. The memory of having been betrayed tends to make me melodramatic.) Tim hobbles toward me. We embrace. We are still closely bound, attached, although the cord has long since been replaced, first by the streams of milk from my breasts, and now by his drool, which has attached itself in an uncertain silver string to my sweater. I feel a terrible warmth for everyone in this room. I feel as if I'm going to cry. Now I've knelt to the floor and Tim and I are rocking rhythmically together, cheek to cheek, until Karl neatly intervenes with clean diaper and safety pins. I stand up, then go out to the kitchen to start the supper. And as I am cooking I am sending unheard messages to my family:

Cinderella is home again, People! But she is old and inefficient and her mind's on other things. She has sisters, too, millions of sisters, but her sisters are not ugly. Still, because she has feelings of guilt because of where she's been, before the clock strikes twelve to-night she will have confessed all. She got her prince, by the way, and then discovered that that was not the real issue. The shoe didn't even fit. If the shoe fits, the prince said, Wear it. And everyone, their toes shoved together like fat worms inside that questing testing cone of clear glass, tried to pretend it did—but it didn't fit anyone, not even that tricky little liar, Cinderella. Besides, Cinderella only married the prince in order to get away from her mother. Although she also believed (maybe still believes) in love love love. And Cinderella's mother was mean because she wasn't, among other things, liberated. The difficult words here are: *among other things*. Tomorrow, when my position will no doubt have altered yet once again, these words may well loom even larger. In the meantime, there are geometric progressions, Children, even in fairy tales. And for the moment (only for the moment, just for to-day) this story has a moral. The moral lies in what kind of story it is. And the moral is this: If Cinderella and the prince live happily ever after, then this story is a tragedy.

There was a large group of people standing on a
wharf. They all had bouquets of flowers in their hands.
As Kit stood watching them they began one by one to
hand their bouquets to a group of people standing
facing the wharf, standing on a small graphic hump of
land. As more and more of the people on the wharf
handed over their flowers Kit began to have a strange
feeling of anxiety. Finally only one man on the wharf
still had a bouquet. Kit had a sudden fear that something terrible would happen when he handed over
the flowers to the last empty-handed person on the
land. He handed them over and indeed as he did so all
the flowers in the hands of all the people on the land
turned into bouquets of bare branches. "You see!"
thought Kit, and at that moment she woke up.

In the distance she could hear the happy cries of
people swimming, and through the partly opened
door she could see a column of parched grass and the
flag-pole with its flag hanging limply down. It was very
hot. But why was she here? Why had she been asleep?
Why wasn't she down at the waterfront being lifeguard? Then she remembered that Dirk had sent her
to lie down, telling her that he would take over for
her. After lunch she had felt that tight coiled pain
high up on one side of her head and she had felt as if
she might throw up. She had told Dirk she thought
she had a migraine coming on. "Go and lie down,

then," he had said, "I'll take over your job." Still she had felt reluctant, Dirk was always so decent. "What's the matter?" he had asked her, "don't you think I can swim?" "Of course I know you can swim." "Well, go on then, or do you want me to carry you to bed?" That had scared her, and she had hurried off, had taken some aspirin, had ducked into her bottom bunk bed and must have immediately fallen asleep. Now she wakened to the sounds of swimming, to the smells of wet bathing caps and rubber sheets (she was a counsellor for a cabin of six-to-eight-year-old bed-wetters) and to the sight, there on the floor, of her still-wet bathing-suit, inside-out, its twisted crotch embedded with rivers of sand. She rubbed at the small coil of pain, which had at least not got any worse. She looked around the cabin, so strangely quiet, free of its complement of little boys. Boys without homes, boys without mothers, boys who peed in the night.

On the outside of the cabin, over the door, was a weatherbeaten sign carved with the words, THE SONS OF SATAN. After nights spent mediating violent fights and mornings spent heaving wet mattresses around in the sun she sometimes wondered if the sign was in fact true. But the Sons of Satan were endearing in many ways and they had given her many things, not least of them the status of having the most difficult cabin in the whole camp. On the inside of the cabin there were many things written on the walls—from the time of the expensive boys' camp that used the place in July. Some things written, some things carved. MARGY T. SMELLS LIKE HER THING someone had carved, laboriously but with terrible succinctness. And one enterprising person had written: EVERYTHING WRITTEN ON THESE WALLS WAS WRITTEN BY ME. Signed: JAMES OLSEN, JR. Kit thought that maybe some of the things written on the wall since that time (James Olsen, Jr. hadn't dated what he wrote) might be things that James

Olsen, Jr. might not want to take responsibility for.

Today was her fourth day at the camp. Yesterday, as she had come into the main lodge on an errand, she had heard Dirk playing his guitar to a group of thirteen-year-olds. "I loved you in the morning . . ." Dirk was singing, "our kisses deep and warm . . . ." Kit hesitated in the sunlit doorway, at least partly aware of the way her fair hair was Botticellied by light, "your hair upon the pillow like a sleepy golden storm . . ." sang Dirk, smiling up at Kit, whose eyes (she was aware of it herself) filled up with alarm, and she went walking by in a bikini that was largely covered with a big blue sweatshirt, so that there was only a small quivering strip of stems and points of petals showing as she went walking by. She opened the screen door on the far side of the lodge and stepped through, as she did so hearing Dirk's rough-edged voice crying, "your eyes are soft with sorrow . . . . Hey that's no way to say good-bye."

She got up from her bunk bed and began to get into her clothes. She took her navy shorts out from the suitcase and also her shocking pink T-shirt. She had absolutely flawless legs—long, brown, perfectly shaped, and she also had good hips, a small waist and a high full bosom. And long fair hair. So far so good. She also had protruding teeth and was nearsighted enough to need glasses. The glasses she carried in her pocket, to be lifted up to her eyes like a double-handled pince-nez in times of emergency. After she had dressed she sat down on the bed again. She still felt a little sick. She thought of Hudsie as she had seen her that morning, pirouetting among the garbage cans, flapping her arms and crying "I feel the winds of Heaven in my sails!" Hudsie was the camp director. At breakfasts, Hudsie was usually in a manic mood. She would sometimes hit her glass with her spoon and in an arch voice order them all to sing absurd songs while they were waiting for their cream of wheat.

Cream of wheat carried in in steaming chipped enamel jugs. Hudsie's favourite absurd song was the national anthem. When she requested it, there would be mutterings, at the counsellors table, of "Good God, our national dirge," and "Hudsie's a sadist! Hudsie's a sadist!" But they would sing it obediently anyway, the children with wide serious eyes, shivering in their thin shorts and T-shirts; the counsellors too sleepy to feel the cold, too tired to prolong the air of parody by seeking each other's eyes. Outside through the open doors the poplar trees would be rattling like millions of little pale green moons and beyond that again the river would be a cold and baleful silver. And at lunchtimes, over coffee, when the women counsellors were sitting around the table together, talking about childhood traumata or the stupidness of politicians, Hudsie would sometimes produce letters and snapshots from her daughters (both student nurses) and these snapshots of blurred girls in pyjamas making cocoa in the nurses' residence would be passed around and the counsellors would murmur politely. Hudsie would usually also give the women counsellors a progress report on "the Hudson River." The Hudson River was Hudsie's menstrual flow (she had reached the menopause) and she told them that she thought of this last prolific menstruation as the extravagant gesture typical of the end of an era. "I have reached the end of an era," she would say, loading her coffee with sugar and looking sly. Hudsie's husband Phil, a tired-looking social worker who came up to the camp from the city on Tuesdays and Fridays, was also in on the act. He always came into camp carrying two large grocery bags—"necessary supplies" he called them—one bag filled with potato chips for "the kids," the other filled with sanitary napkins for "the Hudson River." Hudsie was a paradoxical woman and seemed to enjoy being so. For instance: for two days in a row the cook had presented them with an unusual jello for dessert. It was thriving with spices; bulbed black flecks swam through it (cloves? tadpoles?) and it looked as if it had been made from muddy water. It was very good tasting. On the second day of its appearance, while eating it, Hudsie had been acquainting them all with her progressive views on bringing up children, and had then turned on the cook, whom she usually seemed to like, and said in a to-the-manner-born kind of voice, "Cook, this marvellous jello with all the spices in it is very *nice,* but do you think you might make up a few dozen pans of butterscotch pudding, *just for a little change?*" There was no predicting what Hudsie would do next. Some people loved that, but it made Kit a little nervous.

Dirk and Joe Mazotta had taken the Eight to Tens on a hike in the morning. Now it was near suppertime, the waterfront had been cleared and they sat together on the warm deserted wharf, their feet submerged, the river their foot-bath.

"That lifeguard, that Kit girl, what a body!" groaned Joe Mazotta. "But scared, scared of her own equipment, it's a crime, a body like that, and scared of it."

"She's just shy, Joe."

"A crime, a crime," cried Joe, made sad by lust.

"Maybe you should try to take her out of her shell," Dirk suggested. Immediately he regretted saying this, since Joe's idea of taking a girl out of her shell would probably be to rape her. But Joe surprised him by saying,

"You know how long it would take to take a girl like her out of her shell? Three years at the least."

"Probably," Dirk said.

"After one whole year of talking to her in a quiet voice and never making any sudden unexpected moves you would be allowed to touch her . . . ."

Dirk smiled.

"On the arm," said Joe.

Dirk nodded.

"By accident," said Joe.

Dirk laughed.

"At the end of *two* years," said Joe, "you'd be allowed to hold her hand. But only for *functional* reasons. Like if you were helping her up from a chair or down from a platform or something."

"Yeah," said Dirk.

"At the end of *three* years," said Joe, holding up an index finger, "you'd be allowed to kiss her."

"Don't go too fast, now," Dirk said.

"On the mouth," said Joe.

"It seems to me you're rushing things."

"With her mouth closed," said Joe. "*Jesus!*"

They both laughed. For the thing that had stood out about Kit right away was that she always smiled with her mouth closed. She even seemed to be trying to talk with her mouth closed. Dirk had been puzzled by the fact that he could hardly hear a word she said when the counsellors had all met that first night. Then he had sensed, watching her, a real self-consciousness around the mouth, and she had laughed once, quite spontaneously by accident, and her teeth had popped out from her smile and at once, aware of this, she had quickly closed her mouth. This had reminded Dirk of the times he had been a lifeguard for a group of energetic thirteen- and fourteen-year-old girls. Sometimes in the general athletic abandon, a round white breast would pop out from a bathing-suit, to be at once desperately stuffed back in, great giggling following this, and the girl who'd had the good luck or the bad luck or whatever kind of luck it was to have popped would be the subject of all kinds of jokes and nicknames. "Hey Popsy! Hey Pop-up toaster! Hey Popeye! Hey Pop-something-else! Hey Pop-you-know-what!" they had called with cruel glee, swooning around in the water, probably hoping it would happen to them. "Oh, for heaven's sake!" the girl whose breast had popped out would say, "Don't be so *childish*!" He remembered one statuesque fourteen-year-old who had been a victim of this kind of harassment and how she had finally swum far out into the river trying to retrieve her dignity. A girl called Mary. "Mary, Mary, quite contrary, how does your unh-unh grow!" the other girls had started chanting in their loud excited voices. "Oh for Christ's sake, *swim*!" Dirk had finally yelled, exasperated. "That's what you're here for!" And chastened, they had all gone out to the diving platform, and had practised their diving, trying to knock each other off the platform with their elbows. Mary, though, had been cool and remote with him for a long time after, probably to make sure he understood she hadn't done it on purpose.

At the social night on the second night of camp Dirk had danced with Kit. So had Joe, holding Kit's voluptuous stilted body hard against him, trying to get some life into her through a kind of artificial respiration of the whole body. Dirk too had noticed how stiff Kit was, how her eyes were rather desperately trying not to look desperate, how she wore a social (closed-mouth) smile. On the two social nights that followed, Dirk hadn't asked Kit to dance. Out of simple compassion he hadn't danced with her again. But Joe had kept on trying, shaking in the shaking dances, and drawing her so close to him that she could hardly breathe when they danced to some of Hudsie's old records, things like *The Anniversary Waltz*, which were pretty grim but which came in useful for holding Kit. "Oh how we danced on the night we were wed," Joe sang soft and tender into Kit's golden hair, aware of the hard young eyes of Kit's protector, thirteen-year-old Ralphie Fuente, watching every move he made.

Jeannie Jenner liked Kit. Ever since that morning, over a week ago, when she and Kit had been walking along in the fog from the Main Lodge over to the First Aid Station, she had felt a strong bond with Kit. Jeannie had been feeling nauseated and had suddenly knelt there on the path and started to retch. Kit had dropped to her knees beside her and held her head with one of her cool young hands. Jeannie had vomited until she was weak and Kit had held her head the whole time. Then Kit had walked her, supporting her, into the First Aid Station, covered her with a blanket, given her some gravol and gone back and cleaned up the vomit from the path. Jeannie hoped it wasn't morning sickness that she had. Now, a week later, sitting with Kit in the sun, she was still waiting for proof that it wasn't.

"Poor Hudsie," Kit said, unexpectedly.

"Poor Hudsie my foot," said Jeannie. "Poor everyone else is more like it."

"Well, going through the change of life and all that."

"So? Doesn't everybody? I'll tell you something—she's the only woman I've ever known to make the menopause into a *cause célèbre*." All that talk about bleeding was beginning to get Jeannie down. She wished she would start to bleed herself.

Kit hardly knew what to say. She wasn't sure they should talk about Hudsie this way. After all, Hudsie was their boss.

"Mind you," Jeannie said, "at least 90 percent of all this talk about the Hudson River is just to keep us all entertained. And to keep our minds off the fact that this place is understaffed and she's working us all damn hard."

Hudsie (speak of the devil!) appeared at the far end of the lodge with a leaning tower of folded white towels in her arms.

"Hi, Hudsie!" Jeannie called, "How goes it?"

Hudsie shrugged. "It goes."

"How's the Hudson River?" Jeannie called.

"It flows."

And Hudsie and leaning tower of towels disappeared through the dining-hall doors.

After a short silence Jeannie said, "Any day now Hudsie is going to come down to the waterfront and fall into the river with all her clothes on."

"How do you know that?"

"Because this is my third summer here and she does it every year."

"Why?"

"Because she has an absolute politician's instinct for creating a diversion at the right time. And every summer along about the second week of camp, when there's a general feeling of anti-climax in the air, Hudsie goes down to the waterfront, stands on the wharf, makes sure that everyone's aware she's there, then stumbles and falls into the river. Every summer. Regular as clockwork. With her watch on and everything. She's far too smart to fall in in her bathing-suit. It has to be with the clothes and watch on. That's the only way it's any fun. The little kids love it. She lets them rescue her. They pull her along by the elbows and her hair fans out around her. Real Ophelia stuff."

"I'll be on the lookout for it," Kit said.

"You don't need to be on the lookout for it, the way she does it, it's impossible to miss."

Kit smiled.

"You may think I don't like Hudsie, talking about her this way."

This was exactly what Kit did think.

"Well you're wrong," Jeannie said. "I wouldn't be coming here for the third summer in a row if I didn't like that woman. It's just that it bugs me to hear how protective people feel toward her when she's the shrewdest cookie around."

Noncommittal, Kit continued to shell peas.

Jeannie could see how Kit's diplomatic silences tended to get people down. "Do you agree with me?"

"Yes, I think so," Kit said.

"Take the way she knows I'm sleeping with Dirk, for instance. I know she knows it's going on, my bedroom is right next to hers for Christ's sake, but not only does she not say Boo, she also keeps her radio on till one or two in the mornings so we don't have to worry about bedsprings and things. I mean, *basically*, she's an extremely *kind* person."

Kit was at a loss for words. She hadn't known that about Dirk and Jeannie. She had a terrible sensation of being on the outside of everything, not only on the outside of the things themselves, but on the outside of the knowledge of them. Besides, she had been secretly in love with Dirk for quite a while and had been foolish enough to feel he was secretly in love with her. To herself she recalled primly that she and Dirk were close to the same age, the same height, that they were both lifeguards; that Jeannie was too old for him, too tall and not a lifeguard and she was forced to see that none of this mattered in the slightest. "Dirk rather likes *you*, you know," Jeannie said with a generous lack of tact.

The thought that they had been discussing her (probably in bed) alarmed Kit.

"Oh well, Dirk is very nice," Kit said, hopeless and casual.

"You're damn right he is," said the girl who was in a position to know.

And that afternoon, right on schedule—it was the end of the second week of camp—Hudsie stumbled on the wharf and fell into the river with all her clothes on. It made Kit feel sad, maybe because it seemed to prove that that thing about Dirk and Jeannie Jenner was true.

After the waterfront was cleared at five o'clock, Kit always stayed behind to collect the forgotten things. Ralphie always stayed too, walked along with her, helped her pick up bathing-caps and towels and comic books and sunglasses. Then Kit usually went out for a last swim while Ralphie sat patiently on the wharf and waited for her.

One evening when she had swum out very far—it had been an extremely hot day and the sun was still very strong on her sunburned face—she was lying out in the middle of the river, on her back, floating, her eyes closed against the late hot sun, when she suddenly felt something near her. She rolled over and started treading water. It was Ralphie. "Whaderya doing way out here, Ralphie?"

"Just thought I'd come out to visit you." Big smile.

God, she could get into trouble for this, the children weren't allowed to swim out beyond the log markers. What if he couldn't make it back, she didn't know if she had strength enough to swim him all the way back in. "I'll swim between your legs," he said, and before she could tell him No, he had sunk beneath the black water. For a moment she had a terrible image of him trying to pry open her legs, and losing his breath and sinking down down into the deep river. It was said to be over a hundred feet deep out here. The lodge looked very small in the distance. The cabins, lost in shade and foliage, she couldn't even see. She opened her legs. She felt the curious wraith-like sensation of his moving through. Then he popped up, otter-like, looking pleased as punch. His St. Christopher medal, which hung on a fine chain around his neck, flashed in the sun. She hoped he wasn't relying on that to get him back to shore.

"Ralphie. . . ."

"Again," he said, and he sank at once beneath the black skin of the water. This time he grazed one of her legs as he went through. But before he emerged she had started stroking out toward land. "Give you a race!" she called. It was the only way she could think of to break up this mid-river flirtation without hurting his feelings. She had had terrible visions of river-dragging operations pulling up this odd couple, this sixteen-year-old girl, this thirteen-year-old boy, this aquatic Romeo and Juliet, this counsellor and her charge. Ordinarily she was a stronger swimmer than Ralphie but she let him win. As a matter of fact her legs felt as powerless as seaweed and she took her time going back. He was waiting there on the wharf and he leaned down and grasped her by the wrists and pulled her up on the platform. In profile, in her bronze bathing-cap, her head looked like Nephertiti's. He took a big towel and dried her down. There was a worried-mother tenderness in the thorough rough way he rubbed her with the towel. She knew it was her duty to tell him that he must never swim beyond the log markers again, but she couldn't bring herself to do it. Carrying the daily haul of forgotten things they walked across the long shadows together toward the lodge and their supper.

Jeannie Jenner appeared in the doorway of the SONS OF SATAN cabin. She was wearing faded blue shorts and a grease-mottled sweatshirt. She had shoved the sleeves up to the elbows of her sunburned arms. The peeling skin looked like flakes of silver; the sun had faded and silvered her various skins—skin of clothes, skin of skin—had given her, in the hall-light of evening, a gently luminous look.

"Hey Kit!" she said, "Do you have any costume jewelry you could lend us for the social evening? Joe Mazotta's going to wear one of the cook's purple dresses and he's going to sing an aria from Puccini."
"I've got a few strings of glass beads, and some drop earrings." In fact it was nice there was finally going to be some use for them, even if they were going to be worn in parody, and by someone else. She wondered if Joe Mazotta would enjoy the feel of her necklace circling his neck, clasping it at the hairy back, if he

would like knowing they were *her* earrings, sparkling like stars and dropping pendants of syrup-coloured glass. She was already planning (even as she was digging around among her clothes trying to find the stuff) how she would take her jewelry over to the pump and pump water down on her necklace and earrings in the darkness, after Joe Mazotta had finished wearing them. She thought of the way he held her when they danced, so tight she could hardly breathe. Dirk's embrace, on the other hand, she imagined would be warm but would still let you be free . . . .

"Dirk and I are going to do a skit," Jeannie said. "He's going to be dressed up as a priest taking confession and I'm the one who's going to confess. I played in the same skit last year, and the counsellor who played the part of the priest was a fellow I was sleeping with at the time." She fell back on one of the bottom bunk beds. "History repeats itself," she said sighing deeply. Happy historian of her own life.

"What are you going to confess?" Kit asked, alarmed.

"Oh nothing real," Jeannie said. "Calm yourself, dear, calm yourself. Just things the kids can identify with. You know, like I say to Dirk, 'Well I stole three cookies from the camp kitchen,' and he says, 'Were they any good?' and I say, 'They were terrible.' This gets a good laugh. Then I say, 'Are you familiar with Mrs. Morrison's cooking?' And he says, 'Unfortunately, yes.' Then I say, 'And I stole some of Hudsie's perfume,' And he says, 'What was it called?' and I say, 'MY SIN.' And then I say 'I stole some money from Hudsie's room, too,' and he says, 'Good for you, my dear, Hudsie's an old skinflint, the only way you'll ever get any money out of her is to steal it.'"

Kit was sitting tailor-style on one of the other lower bunks.

"And what will Mrs. Morrison think of those comments on her cooking? And what will Hudsie think of people making fun of her in front of all the kids?"

"Dear Kit."

"Dear Kit, why? Why Dear Kit?"

"Dear Kit, because Mrs. Morrison loves those comments on her cooking. She knows that she's a very good cook, 80 times better than the cooks they have at Immaculata or at the reform school. Everybody else knows it too. And as for Hudsie being hurt by that skit, I'll tell you something, dear Kit: Hudsie *invented* that skit."

"I see."

"And do you know why?"

"Because she thinks it's healthy for the kids to have a chance to make fun of her?"

"Partly."

"And why else?"

"Because Hudsie is trying to rehabilitate these kids, with the very few primitive means she has at her disposal. It's not enough to let them swim and get fresh air and sunshine and surround them with people who are kind to them. Some of these kids have got criminal convictions, some of these kids feel completely worthless because of the things they've done, so when Hudsie engineers a skit like that, she's saying, 'Most children steal. They steal cookies, for instance, and when they get older they steal perfume, and they sometimes steal money.' And when she has the priest say, 'Hudsie's an old skinflint, the only way you'll ever get any money out of her is to steal it,' she's expressing some of the hostile feelings these kids have, and the way they use them to justify the things they sometimes do, except that the kids know that Hudsie isn't an old skinflint, that she is in fact an extremely generous person, and knowing this they can't always justify their stealing by dismissing the people they're stealing from as being stupid and old and stingy and mean."

"Well it all seems kind of chancy," Kit said.

"But *life* is chancy, Kit!"

There was silence for a few moments, then Jeannie Jenner went on, "if there's anything that these kids here prove, coming as they do from illegitimate unions and broken homes, it's that: life is chancy. In the meantime Hudsie makes do with what she's got. I'll tell you something: When the Children's Aid comes into this camp every August, the expensive boys' camp that was here in July takes away practically everything—the horses, the sailboats, the bows and arrows for archery (presumably that's for our own protection in case the little monsters decide to attack us), even the kilns, for crying out loud, so we can't even teach the underprivileged how to make pottery. Would you believe they actually uproot the kilns and cart them away? So what we have left is Dirk teaching the kids how to make things out of papier mâché and singing folk-songs with them and taking them for nature hikes, and we have Joe Mazotta teaching them judo and taking them for nature hikes, and we have Marion teaching them canoeing and taking them for nature hikes, and we have me teaching them modern dance and patching up their cuts and stings and scratches, and we have you teaching them swimming and being gentle with the little children, and we have Hudsie dreaming up wild entertainments. But I've worked with Hudsie for a long time now, and I know she'll allow unconventional things to happen if she thinks they'll work. Like letting an ex-juvenile delinquent like me sleep with Dirk for instance. Dirk is only seventeen, after all, and here am I, a worn old woman of 28, with an abortion and a drugs charge to my credit, but Dirk and I are valuable counsellors to Hudsie and so she allows us to keep each other happy in the bedroom next to hers."

Kit didn't want to hear about how they kept each

other happy. In the bedroom next to Hudsie's or anywhere else.

"Well, what does Hudsie think of an unconventional arrangement like my friendship with Ralphie Fuente, then? I suppose she thinks it's *cute*."

Kit was feeling very defensive.

"Hudsie wouldn't be apt to dismiss any kind of real relationship between two people as being 'cute,' I'm sure you realize that."

"What does she think it is, then?"

"My guess would be—and this is only a guess, mind you—my guess would be that she think's it's therapeutic." Jeannie hesitated, then plunged wholly in. "For both of you," she said.

Kit waited.

"Look at Ralphie Fuente, he's got a list of convictions as long as your arm. Hanging around with you has probably done him a lot of good, but hasn't it done you some good too? I mean, it's not just a one-way thing, is it, luv? And that's the thing about Hudsie, she doesn't divide people up into good and bad and sick and well and criminal and responsible and adults and children." She hesitated, a little doubtful. "At least she doesn't usually. Not that I agree with all her techniques—some of them are just pure sensation-mongering, she can be a phony, and she can be an exhibitionist, and she can confuse people pretty badly sometimes, I guess, and she's tedious as hell about her bloody Hudson River, but I've been hard on her about that because I've been waiting for a bit of Hudson River myself." "She seems like an unhappy person to me," Kit said. "All that activity all the time. I know you think that all the talk and activity is a diversionary tactic to keep everybody's minds off what's wrong with this place but maybe it's also a diversionary tactic to keep her own mind off what's wrong with herself."

"*Kit*!"

"What?"

"You're being quite hard on dear old Hudsie."

Kit sat silent.

"I think what you're saying is true, though, for Chissake, don't start feeling guilty." Jeannie stretched. "Still, she's quite a remarkable old girl in her way. She's going to be singing, *I'm Just a Girl Who Can't Say No*, by the way, going to get herself all gussied up in gingham and lace. That should be *my* song, shouldn't it, but I'm going to be singing *Un Canadien Errant* with a bunch of the kids. Ah, those convent voices! Clear as crystal! Dirk's going to sing *If I Were a Carpenter* and Phil Hudson's going to sing one of those animal songs that has lots of snorts and farts in it." She paused, considering. "Can you sing, Kit?"

"No," said Kit, "can't sing."

Even only being a spectator at these social evenings sometimes depressed Kit. She would sometimes slip away early and walk in the dark up to her cabin—the flashlight feeding the path down to her in eerie abrupt little humps. And very soon she would be lying in her bunk surrounded by sleeping Sons of Satan and dreaming her waking dreams of lovers.

And at the end of the social evening as Dirk was singing, "If I were a carpenter and you were a lay-dee, would you marry me anyway . . . would you have my bay-bee?" Ralphie Fuente put his arm around Kit's shoulder. She put her arm around his waist. A list of convictions as long as your arm, she was thinking, not that she hadn't known from the very beginning about Ralphie's past. It was just that she had always felt so happy from the good she was doing him. "I gave you my onlyness . . ." sang Dirk, "give me your tomorrow . . . ."

Ralphie's hand was cupped around the warm smooth hump of her shoulder. The thought that Ralphie was also doing *her* some good puzzled Kit, and she put it out of her mind. As for Jeannie Jenner her menstrual

period had begun the day before. Last night Dirk
had come in to be with her anyway, to keep her warm
and to rub the cramps out of her belly. They had both
nearly cried with relief. So now she could relax sitting
there in her serape, and simply find the song moving.
All the same (and that's ambivalence for you, she was
thinking), the whole time Dirk was singing it, she
never once took her eyes off his beautiful face.

The Immaculata Orphanage looked like something
out of a story by one of the Brontës, especially now
in frozen, grey, bare-branched December. Playing-
fields of frozen mud bounded the cracked concrete
walk on either side and the long dark red-brick building
had rows and rows of dark windows without curtains,
only here and there a partly pulled white window
blind. Kit had walked the considerable distance from
the bus depot with her two giant-sized paper bags that
were filled with toys for Christmas. In her wildest
dreams she couldn't have asked for a more depressing
institution to offset the newness and colour she carried
there in her shopping bags, for the bags were filled
with $75 worth (her whole three-weeks' salary from
the Children's Aid Camp) of red and turquoise plastic
that was moulded into slinkies and trucks, of maroon
rubber monsters with seaweed-like feet, of dolls,
kites, science kits, and chemistry sets. Now the summer camp seemed eons ago. Dirk, Ralphie, Jeannie
Jenner and Joe Mazotta had all gone their separate
ways and Kit had been back at the high school for three
long sad months. She had lost contact with all of them,
with Dirk and Joe who'd gone heaven knows where,
with Ralphie Fuente who was, she had heard, at some
halfway house, with Jeannie Jenner, who had gone
inland—to Montreal or Toronto—to work with drug
addicts. The time at the camp seemed a golden age,
never to come again. All she'd had left of it was the
$75 that she'd put into a bank account when the camp

had closed the first week in September. She hadn't spent the money on clothes for school. The money had remained there intact, all that was left of what now seemed a perfect summer. Then sometime in November it had occurred to her she should do something with it, and having had a thunderbolt of inspiration, she had gone immediately to the bank, taken it all out, closed the account, taken the money to a department store where she had spent every last cent of it on toys for the orphans of Immaculata. For two weeks the bags sat in her bedroom, reassuring her and making her happy. The night of the class dance at school . . . she hadn't gone to that . . . she had gone up to her room after supper and taken out all the toys and spread them all over the bed and desk and dresser and chairs, had turned on the low lamps at the tables and flooded her treasures with light, had stood like a miser contemplating jewels.

And now here she was at the orphanage, ringing the bell. A novice appeared at the door and took her up a long dark flight of stairs to see the nun who ran the orphanage—an institution herself, according to Hudsie's stories—an old woman called Sister St. Patrick.

"Would you please wait here," the novice said. "If you'd like to sit down, Sister St. Patrick will be in to see you very soon."

Kit was left alone in a small room with a couple of chairs and a desk. The walls were white and there were several crucifixes on them, of varying sizes. Some of the Christ-figures were ivory and some of them were gold. Some of the crosses were black, some of them were brown. Kit's mouth felt dry and she kept crossing and re-crossing her ankles. "Very kind of you, very kind indeed," said the old Sister St. Patrick when she heard why Kit was there. The orphanage was often on the receiving end of various small charitable acts, and for all these charitable acts the sister said her magic words, Very kind, very kind.

She led Kit along a labyrinth of dark halls. Here and there in the hallways there were drawings of the crucifixion or of the madonna and child, which had attained, brown with age and under glass, the quality of old photographs. There was the noise of children playing in one of the halls above them. Sister St. Patrick paused in the stairwell.

"Children!" she called. A group of them appeared along the high bannister, and stood looking down.

"Look who's here," Sister St. Patrick said.

The children looked.

Kit looked hopefully back. In fact she couldn't immediately recognize these faces who—unlike the drawings gone brown with age—had lost the brown of summer and had become white with the passing of time. One or two faces looked vaguely familiar but out of their bathing-suits and in their dark tunics she couldn't be sure. There were no Sons of Satan among them anyway. From the railing the children looked down, equally perplexed. Many people came and went in their lives.

"See," Sister said, "she's brought you some toys. Lots and lots of toys. Now isn't that kind?"

There was then some whispering among the children, and some arguing back and forth. "The one with the *buck teeth*," someone said finally in a stage whisper, clinching it. "*You know*," the same voice whispered, "the one they called *Rabbit*." "The swimming teacher!" cried another voice in a shrill whisper. "Oh yeah," said a third voice, normal-level, enlightened, "now I remember."

"You can go back to play now, children," Sister said in a rather high voice. She turned to Kit with a face that was doubly apologetic. Apologetic for the fact that she hadn't been able to weed the original apology from her very pale old face. "We'll go and visit the nursery," she said. And she descended the stairs ahead of Kit to give the poor child time to pull herself together. She wished terribly that she had thought of the nursery in the first place, the nursery was the obvious place with all its clinging toddlers who greeted perfect strangers like long-lost friends.

"I never did get up to visit the camp where the children go," Sister said, deliberately making casual conversation, "but they tell me it's very beautiful there. What's the name of that river, where the camp is?"

"The Hudson River," Kit said.

"Ah yes. And a very nice person Mrs. Hudson is too."

"Yes," said Kit, "she is."

They continued to descend into a world of cries and cooking-smells.

"But I made a mistake about the river!" Kit called to Sister St. Patrick. "The *river* is called the *Nerepis River*!" She remembered the boys in cabin 8 chanting:

Here a pis, There a pis,
Hey! Hey! Hey!
Nerepis, Nerepis,
Yay! Yay! Yay!

"It's an Indian name," Kit said, somehow feeling responsible for it and so trying to cancel out its bathroom quality.

But Sister St. Patrick seemed not to hear, seemed to be thinking about Mrs. Hudson. "Hudsie, they call her, don't they?" she asked Kit.

"Yes."

They had reached it now if the noise was anything to go by. There was a cacophonous sound from behind the frosted-glass doors.

"We are more than filled to capacity. We should issue visitors with ear-plugs," Sister said, and then could have bitten her tongue out. She left Kit with some children near the door and hurried over to speak for a few minutes to the young sister in charge.

Many of the younger children seemed in some way to remember Kit; they perhaps didn't remember her from any specific place or time but they at once garlanded themselves around her hips and hung three and four to each arm, feeling her as something long ago felt and leaned to, and beautifully impeding her movements. At that moment it would have been easy for her to cry from happiness since she was already nearly crying from something else.

After Sister St. Patrick had gone ("How can we ever thank you?" she had asked Kit before going. It was a statutory question), the children started agitating to have the presents. "No," the young nun in charge said sharply, "not till Christmas." Along with the Reverend Mother she wished people would just give money if they wanted to help. Besides, she had a terrible cold. The base of her nose was raw and the nostrils were almost translucent. She had sequestered whole flocks of kleenex high up in her wide sleeves and now and then pulled some out, like a magician pulling out silk scarves. Her head ached terribly.

Kit was being herded by a group of young children to various points of interest in the room. Someone wanted her to look at his paintings, someone else wanted her to see the hamsters. They were all fighting to have her look at things they'd made or been given. And "Hi, Kit!" a boy's voice suddenly said. Kit turned. It was one of the Sons of Satan. "Hi!" Kit said, "How are *you*?" but he ducked shyly through the children and quickly disappeared. Kit knew that her presents had been put away somewhere to be absorbed by that vast anonymous sea of gifts that would be coming from the Knights of Columbus and other organizational groups. There was nothing more to do.

"What's the quickest way out?" she asked the young nun.

"You didn't want to see Sister St. Patrick again, then?"

"Well, no, I wouldn't like to bother her, I really must run anyway, I have a bus to catch, and there's something I've promised to be back in town for at five o'clock." She was overdoing it, giving too many reasons. And none of them true. It seemed strange that she had once planned to spend the whole afternoon here, perhaps even staying for supper.

"Well, if you turn left at the end of that hallway and walk a little piece you'll come to a stairway that'll let you out one of the side entrances."

Kit thanked her, waved good-bye to the children, walked along the hall and found the stairway. Once outside she buttoned up her coat and tied on her dark tartan wool bandana. She wiped her eyes with the back of her hand and put on her glasses, then her brown wool gloves. Under her coat, under her layers of sweaters, she could feel how her nipples were going erect, but only from the cold. She had managed not to run into Sister St. Patrick again, anyway, she should be grateful for small mercies. In fact not running into Sister St. Patrick again gave her the sensation of having had a narrow escape. She could see how cruelly Sister St. Patrick's kind gaze would have set the seal on her humiliation. But that was only a narrow escape in the narrow sense. In the broader sense she could feel how she had also had a narrow escape. She was thinking about Hudsie talking about the Hudson River, was remembering Hudsie saying that the profuse menstruation of the menopause was the extravagant gesture signalling the end of an era. She kept thinking about the Hudson River as she continued to walk slowly, steadily toward the bus stop. She had to force herself to keep moving. One foot after the other. Left. Right. Toys. Blood. Left. Right. Toys. Blood. All the spirit seemed to have been drained out of her.

OUR LADY OF ALL THE DISTANCES

She sometimes thought of Sam up there. She had one image of the northern summer—an image of tawny moth-eaten tundra, like a faded golden carcass partly eaten away by mud, and above it, rising forever, a shimmering pale sky. All the movies, all the slides, all the black-and-white stills—all the shots of sea-planes tethered to fallen wharves, caught against blinding northern lakes, blinding northern suns—that Sam had brought back with him over the years had done nothing to alter it. And in any case her image was her own cliché, and therefore a better cliché than ice and snow.

She had an image for Sam, too (in case he didn't have one of his own), of them, his family, far to the south of him, part of a congested untidy human tide-mark on the lower part of the sandy stretch of Mooney's Bay. And although fewer and fewer Americans came to Canada for their summer vacations with skis on the tops of their cars, few of them could have imagined the oppressive Texan-like heat through which she now led her two young sons as they worked their way to the water's edge.

She wished she had worn a big loose dress for her ordeal of walking through the sun-bathers to the beach. Her big white vulnerable thighs quivered, testy in anticipation of second looks. But there would be no second looks. There would be no first looks.

It had been years since there had been second looks and almost as many since there had been first looks. Her children followed her, each according to his own style. Billie, four, walked eagerly toward the water, his friend. Shaun, seven, a first child (and because of that? because of her? because of what?), walked near her—as if leashed to her own ennui—sour, complaining about all the things it was not in her power to change—that it was too hot, that the walk to the beach was too long, that he was tired, that he wished he hadn't come.

On the terrace of the cabana they paused a moment, paused like far-eyed conquerors, and looked out over the prone bazaar of the beach with all its people felled by sun. People who had transistor radios were there. In force. They lay in little groups on their tight bellies with their Tahitian-flower-blooming bums beamed at the sun. Even to her their eyes seemed too hard, too level, aimed as impersonally as artillery above their jarring fortresses of sound. Shaun, in skirting distrustfully around one of these groups, inevitably came into the radius of another almost exactly like it, and the beach seemed to her then a parody of life itself, an endless plain of overlapping circles, and backing out of one, you backed into another, which, if not the same, was probably worse. Oh, she was in a bad mood today, she really and truly was.

They passed by a whole colony of single girls, falsely bright single girls, wearing wrap-around sunglasses and lying like burnt offerings on their giant Aztec beach-towels, and farther down they passed a woman whose radio sang-growled: "Zank 'eaven for leetle girls, zey grow up in zee most delightful way." The woman had caressed herself with oil till her skin shone wetly. She was past the age where she had grown up in the most delightful way, but she seemed to have taken good care of herself all the same; her hair was protected by a smart little head scarf, and her beach-coat—thrown down to one side of her—was made of an impressive fabric, like one of Rousseau's paintings of dreams.

Nearer the water's edge were the young gods and goddesses, and they were so perfect that she could hardly bear to look. They had perfect overall tans. Only when they laughed, only when they bent over in their young convulsive way could you glimpse small winter white slits of skin. She herself had a housewife's tan that came from wearing high-necked sleeveless dresses, so that her legs were tanned below the knee and her arms up to the shoulder, but there was a vast expanse around her bathing-suit that was a slack and sick-room white. And there were a few workmen's tans—tanned torsos, white legs—and there was one alarming man who had one white leg, one brown one. When she noticed that he walked with a limp, she realized that his harlequin look came from his having recently worn a cast.

She settled herself down and got out the children's things. On her beach-bag a stylized blue flounder swam through perfect waves of turquoise rick-rack. Christmas-present beach-bag. And very useful it was turning out to be, too, here on the burning glitter of the sands of summer. She sighed, dispensing pails and warships.

For a while she watched the lifeguards, solid and visored on their wooden towers, their whistles twinkling like lockets in the sun. And there were the people nearby who had brought their terrible efficiency to the beach with them, and who now produced an incredible assortment of containers in plaid vinyl and primary-coloured plastics. She thought she remembered them from last year. She thought she remembered their equipment.

Farther down, Billie squatted at the water's start, gouging the wet sand with his pail. Shaun stood close by, disinterested, tense. Such desperate apathy reminded her of her own childhood, but did not make her sympathetic. She narrowed her eyes against the pewter glare of the water, took out her book, *Encounters with British Intellectuals*, a book she would not be ashamed to leave face-down on the towel when later she went in for a swim. As if anyone cared, she thought, smiling her private smile. She dug a little hole in the wet sand, leaned over, smelled it, decided to use it as an ashtray. Perhaps she had better oil herself before her encounter with the British intellectuals. She ferreted around blindly in her beach-bag for the spill-free container, found it, absently and patchily rubbed oil on herself while she watched her children. At last she began to read.

The afternoon wore on. Serious children's construction work was going on along the sandcastle-line, but nine times out of ten the castles were smashed by huge boys chasing thuddingly after girls who had thrown sand in their faces in the first place. The builders of the castles squatted bewildered, their droopy wet bathing-suits sugared with sand, but soon began again to firm up their cumbled dreams. The sad but patient children made her think of people in bombed cities. She was having a bad day. She was only seeing the sad things. But then the happy things didn't seem to make her feel any better either. Lovers lying nearby didn't cheer her up, only brought to the surface the thought that she had expected more from this trip to the beach than merely giving her children a swim. Reading her book, *trying* to read her book, she was sometimes disturbed by a wincing deep inside her. She lit her cigarette and with her match-stick scratched I WANT deep in the dark sand. But she couldn't finish it, what it was she wanted, even though she had always known what a good censor sand is, had known since she was very young how with one swoop you could smear out the legend of a wish in the sand and no-one would ever know what the wish had been. Sand was even better than snow, that way. She erased I WANT thoroughly, what she wanted being for some lean intelligent man to lower himself down on the blanket beside her. To begin with the book, but to end with her.

On the shoreline there was a casual parade of girls. They came in twos, usually in bikinis, sometimes smoking, plowing the shallow water with their feet. They had made their unawareness of admiring glances almost an art. Watching them, watching the men they promenaded for but pretended not to notice, she wondered if liaisons were formed here. She could not see that they were. And yet at that moment, one of the walking girls, hands on first-rate hips, stopped below the lifeguard's tower and called up to him. He leaned out like a shy king, gesticulating, pointing, describing. The girl winced uncomprehendingly for the noise of the swimmers was truly (and conveniently) deafening. The lifeguard climbed down from his wooden tower, put a protective arm around her, pointed, explained. Yes, liaisons were made, then, and all that walking was not in vain. She sighed, envious, contemptuous, and then suddenly, panic-stricken, tried with her eyes to search out her own children. She found them at last. Shaun seemed after all to be having a happy day, was talking to two similar-sized children, and Billie was on some touching secret mission, still gouging out wet sand with his pail, still tottering to a chosen spot on the lower beach to dump it, still rushing back in a desperate serious way for more, from down where the water made its mindless bright beginning. A tremendous tenderness for him made her throat tense up, bound all the stalks of vocal cords and tendons tightly together.

After a while she called the children in to get something to eat. They sat caped in towels, eating quietly, watching everything. She herself had forgotten, over the winter, so many of the sounds of the river, the interweaving of screams and giggling, the shouts of the young men, the quick way the water throttled their laughter. Not far from them, three boys were wrestling a girl in a yellow blouse and blue jeans toward the water. This had happened every single time she had come to this beach. The same moves. The same counter-moves. Only the players changed.

"Don't!" the girl in blue jeans screamed, loving every minute of it. Her elbows were held high and jutted out, her body was arched back and she dug her heels protestingly into the sand as they dragged her waterwards. Phony, phony, phony. They got her into it thigh high. "Stop it!" she shrieked happily, in her element. "Don't you dare throw me in!" They threw her in. She bobbed up, a happy, vicious, flustered Venus, and started flailing them all with great silver sails of water. Shaun and Billie watched, missing no detail. And through the tea-coloured glass of her sun-glasses she also watched—but with a jaundiced eye.

After food they went back to play and she went back to her book. Some time later, the sky darkened, and she turned her attention away from the river and toward the grass where some people were playing volleyball. There was a Negro girl in a dark green tartan bathing-suit and a girl with long brown hair who had on a bikini that had designs on it like black and brown Japanese brush strokes. Oh, to be young again, she thought, watching them. And yet when she had been young, she had not been like them—she had never been any good at games, she had been an awkward sideliner always, thinking that life would come with being grown-up, just as she now seemed to think it went with being young. Nothing went with anything! When would she ever learn that? It was all part of the mustard with hotdog myth! It was all part of the love with marriage myth! Her mother had been a great believer in that one. And yet it must be wrong to teach your children that life was a series of inevitable and beautiful combinations. Whatever else it *was*, life was not *that*. And it was busy proving it to you twenty times a day. She called her children in to get dressed.

The afternoon was slanting across itself by the time they went to catch their bus. And when they got home their house smelled closed-in, sour. They would have to get some breezes through it. After she had opened the kitchen window, a marvellous ribbon of late summer wind blew through the house; she could feel it on one of her bare shoulders as she stood watching over the bean-sprouts and hamburger heaving and bubbling in the frying pan. She was remembering when she had been a nurse. She had not been a good nurse, and she had been grateful when Sam had come out of the North and rescued her. In some ways she had been too smart to be a nurse, in other ways not smart enough. She seemed never to have got the knack of distances, an important thing for a nurse to get the knack of. There were two kinds of distances, she now realized—the distance that had to be gauged when you raised frail shoulders with one arm while with the other arm you eased in under them with a great cool wedge of hospital pillow, or when you pivoted a 200-pound patient on its quivering axis while with your other hand you did some kind of sleight-of-hand with the bed linen, making it taut as a trampoline. That was one kind of distance, and a kind she had been clumsy with. Then there was the other kind, the emotional kind, and there too her gauging had been out of kilter. Caring too much (or so she had then thought), lifting the frail shoulders with one arm, she had sometimes banged the fat hospital pillow into the wobbling damp head, in her terrible clumsy anxiety to relate, to care. It was the cool-eyed ones (who thought of it as a job) who did it all best. And for the first time it occurred to her that the two distances were interdependent, more interdependent than mustard and hotdogs, more interdependent than love and marriage. She was remembering when she had worked in the delivery room. A happy place where birth was the rule. But there had been a death while she worked there, a death she still remembered. Except to think of it as a death was perhaps inaccurate—and certainly melodramatic—since it was a death-before-birth, the spontaneous abortion of a three- or four-month-old fetus. It was strange she could remember it so clearly. There must have been many similar cases. It was around five o'clock in the morning, she had been cleaning up the utility room to make it ready for the day-shift, and it lay there among all the debris of birth—among all the other things to be flushed away, among the uprooted placentas, the umbilical cords that looked like telephone cords, among the clots like shiny wine-dark jelly, there it was, this pre-human that looked more like a plant than a human being, that looked, in fact, like a bloated white sprouting bean. She stirred the bean-sprouts in the frying pan, acknowledging them as a source of her rememberings. And in the wards beyond the delivery room there was a curious paradox, one that she now remembered. To the left corridor had been the public mothers—the poor ones—to the right had been the middle- and upper-class mothers. And it was in the public ward that you heard loud scientific discussions on the merits of various kinds of anesthetics and formulas—twilight sleep versus spinals, Carnation milk versus soy—whereas in the private wards almost all the mothers had gone primitive, were having natural childbirth, were breastfeeding and spoke no jargon at all. And she remembered some of the shy rich mothers, backed by their ribboned florists' jungles, the way they jerked like startled gazelles at the first hard pull of the baby's mouth on the nipple. Then a conversation she had had with Sam just before he went away. He had been listing the attractions of Eskimo women. And he had been telling her that the highest honour an Eskimo host could pay a visitor (and there would be a lot of settlements where Sam would be a visitor) was to lend his wife to his guest for the night. She had heard those wife-lending stories before. Hot tales from the cold North.

"But do they still do that, now that they're living in all those pre-fab houses?"

"Men lend their wives in pre-fab houses *here* don't they?" he had said, "right in our very own suburbs."

She had sat silent, thinking of Sam and the Eskimo women. "But what about *me*?" she had cried at last, sitting cross-legged on the immense white plain of their bed, "What am I supposed to do while you're away?"

"Fuck yourself," Sam had said, testing the straps of his knapsack.

Now the children were in bed. Not that they had settled to sleep. Well, Shaun had, obliterating the whining day with some tender and original remark that she could not now recall. But with Billie the day could not be so easily given up.

"Come into my room!" he now called, imperious, seductive.

"I've already been to your room twice," she pointed out firmly, from her white haven in the bathroom.

"I've something to tell you."

"Tell it from there."

"Can you hear me?"

One two three testing. "I can hear you," she said.

"I have a riddle for you."

"Alright, ready," she said.

"What colour is a tired elephant?"

She knew this was her cue to play stupid, to incite his joyful, incredulous four-year-old laughter, to guess "chocolate purple" or "Macintosh plaid," but she was too tired. A tired elephant. "Grey," she said.

"Do you give up?"

"I give up."

"Grey," he said.

"Good," she said, briskly, "Now good-night, Billie. No more talking."

"No more talking?" He was cunning as an 83-year-old.

"Big day tomorrow!" she called, trying to make her voice robust with encouragement.

"Mummie?"

"Yes, Billie?" Even her blood seemed to sag in her veins.

"Just come into my room for only one more time?" Sweet and plaintive.

"*Billie*, I *can't* come, I'm doing pooh." This was an activity he had some respect for. Sometimes it took him almost an hour to do it himself. And in what she hoped was a kind but firm voice she said: "Good-night now, darling."

"Good-night, darling," he said.

After five minutes of silence, she went quietly down the hallway to her own room. Outside, darkness was slowly taking charge of the streets, the city's sky. Night fed the shadows. She could imagine lovers, on the slopes of parks, on the slopes of car-seats, being felled by darkness. She turned on the bedside lamp and jolted the outside world (what was left of it) into night. She worked her feet out from her warped sandals and sat on the edge of the bed, looking sideways at a fashion magazine. The pages flapped heavily by. Fashion models wearing white satin dresses were posed against black skies, Brontë landscapes. On one page a girl peered into a seething pool of her own hair—or what appeared to be her own hair—and there were many pages of thick stockings that looked as if tractors had been driven over them, stockings being worn by girls who strode clear-eyed through streets and fields. But out of the corner of her eye, it was the poetry that caught her. All the poems were made up of simple words, words she knew, yet words made to pyramid strangely—into joy, into pain. And although she couldn't always understand the poetry, she felt certain that the poetry *understood her*. That gave her a strange feeling. She closed the magazine and looked up to one wall that had on it a handsome photograph of an arctic church. Taken by Sam. It looked like a Byzantine igloo, something clever had been done with translucent bricks, for the impression you got was of the muted struggle of light shining dimly through thick blocks of snow. She had named this photograph "the Basilica of the Frozen Blood." She got up and went over and looked at herself in the curly gilt-framed mirror. All around the mirror—for contrast—Sam had pasted a photo-collage of Eskimo faces—fine, tough Eskimo faces squinting against an unseen sun. So surrounded, she stood watching herself comb her fair dull hair. For a while she thought of Sam's North and imagined the jarring squeak of boats grating against wood wharves, and waiting on the wharves, men with hair like fur, men wearing the blurred blue plaids of much-washed flannel shirts. Then for no reason that she could think of, she suddenly remembered the one attractive man she had seen at the beach that day, a man who had squatted gently by a small girl at the water's edge. They had stayed there together for some time, the man squatting, the little girl (how old? two?) with that pronounced pregnant-looking stomach that very small girls usually have, and her hands clasped high on it, looking peacefully out at the swimmers. A pot-bellied Renaissance child in a bright red bathing-suit. She had found the father and child curiously touching. And even from that distance, beached on her towel, she had almost felt she was there with them, feeling with them the warm gift and retreat of water lapping at her feet. After a while, and again for no reason that she could fathom, she began to cry. The day had pyramided like the poetry. She was on the painful point. She would have to let herself cry. So she did not sniff it back or wipe at it. It was the beginning of something that she could feel how she was caught in the skein of all the distances. It was the beginning of something that she could cry. There were beginnings here that must be honoured.

And with her bare feet planted on the flowered carpet in the high bright bedroom in the summer night she stood there crying on and on while the Eskimo faces squinted politely all around her.